A SAVIOR FOR BRANWEN

WELSH REBELS

VIRGINIE MARCONATO

OLIVERHEBERBOOKS

All rights reserved.

No part of this publication may be sold, copied, distributed, reproduced or transmitted in any form or by any means, mechanical or digital, including photocopying and recording or by any information storage and retrieval system without the prior written permission of both the publisher, Oliver Heber Books and the author, Virginie Marconato, except in the case of brief quotations embodied in critical articles and reviews.

PUBLISHER'S NOTE: This is a work of fiction. Names, characters, places, and incidents either are the product of the author's imagination or are used fictitiously. Any resemblance to actual persons, living or dead, business establishments, events, or locales is entirely coincidental.

A Savior for Branwen Copyright 2025 © Virginie Marconato

Cover art by Dar Albert at Wicked Smart Designs

Published by Oliver-Heber Books

0 9 8 7 6 5 4 3 2 1

Prologue

She had kissed him.

She had kissed *him*, not the other way around.

Branwen touched her lips lightly, where the faint taste of virile male and spice lingered. Why had she done such a thing? What had happened to her? She did not kiss men, ever! She hated men, she hated the feel of their lips against hers, the heat of their tongues invading her mouth, the possessiveness of their hands roving over her body.

She hated everything about them.

And yet she had kissed Matthew Hunter, here in the solar, for all to see.

It might be that he would have kissed her first if she had not pre-empted it. It was a possibility she could not dismiss out of hand. There had been desire dancing in his eyes, and he had leaned in toward her more than was proper, but she couldn't be sure he would have actually kissed her. Usually she waited until there was no other choice, until she knew she couldn't escape before she resigned herself to letting a man kiss her. But with Matthew ...

With Matthew she had been unable to resist.

Why him?

It wasn't as if he were a friend she had known all her life and trusted not to cross a boundary, or a meek, unassuming man who made her feel safe in her ability to refuse him her favors at the last moment if need be. No, he was not a friend, but a stranger, an Englishman who despised Welsh people, and there was nothing meek or unassuming about him. Quite the opposite. He was the epitome of the man who liked to be in charge, who tumbled women into bed whenever the urge seized him, who didn't wait for their agreement before pouncing, who did not allow his lovers to make the first move.

And yet that was exactly what he'd done with her.

He'd let her decide what would happen.

And it had taken her little more than a heartbeat to decide that what would happen would be a scorching kiss, the likes of which she had never thought she could or would want to share with anyone.

What would have happened if her friend Esyllt's daughter and stepdaughter had not walked in on them? Surely she would have come back to her senses and pushed him away? Surely she wouldn't have demanded more, here in the middle of Castell Esgyrn?

Unfortunately, she couldn't be sure.

One thing was certain, however. She could not afford to see him again, or at least, not alone. If she kept out of the way for a few days, he might well go back to England. His brother Connor, Lord Sheridan, regularly sent him on missions there. Perhaps it would not be long before he asked him to go again? Should she ask Esyllt to suggest to her husband that their English estate needed checking? Yes, perhaps.

Then her moment of folly would be forgotten.

Chapter One

Wales, February 1297

"Are we going to talk about what happened the other day, then?"

To give herself time to restore her composure, Branwen selected an almond from the silver dish in front of her. She wasn't fooled by her friend's attempt at nonchalance, nor could she claim ignorance of what she was alluding to. Her kiss with Matthew. She had hoped to keep it a secret, but obviously the little girls had delighted in revealing to their parents what they had seen. It was to be expected, as was the fact that Esyllt wanted to know more.

The only problem was, Branwen didn't want to talk about it. She had spent the last week trying to push it out of her mind, pretending it had not happened. In vain. Every time she closed her eyes she saw Matthew's perfect face hovering over hers. She saw it as it had appeared just before she'd pushed herself onto her tiptoes to take his mouth in a kiss such as she had never experienced before.

"I didn't think there was any need to talk about it," she said, taking a bite of the treat Esyllt's husband had procured in distant London to satisfy his wife's craving for all things sweet.

It was an extravagant gesture, but nothing was too dear for the woman he loved, especially when she was carrying his child, and as a consequence, could only abide to eat certain things.

When the taste hit her tongue, Branwen almost moaned out loud. Not because it was delicious, even if it was, but because it reminded her of Matthew's kiss. He had tasted just as enticingly spicy as the sweet. Perhaps he'd been eating one of them before she'd captured his mouth in an uncharacteristically daring move.

"No, perhaps there's no need to talk about it," Esyllt agreed, helping herself to another almond. "After all, there are only so many reasons why two people might kiss, all of which I can guess on my own. But don't you wish to—"

"No." Branwen swallowed the almond with difficulty. Was everything and everyone determined to remind her of the man she was trying to forget? "I'm sorry, I cannot talk about it, not when he's your brother-in-law," she added more amenably. She hadn't meant to snap thus, but the conversation was making her feel quite wretched, because the more she thought about it, the more she regretted the kiss. It could only lead to complications.

There was a pause while her friend chewed on her almond.

"Then I will say only this. Be careful with Matthew. He's a good man, but he can be quite possessive and he might not like to hear about ..." Esyllt floundered, clearly at a loss as to how to word her advice without offending her. "Well, I'm not sure he would like to be told of the other men—"

"Yes," Branwen cut in again, understanding all too well.

Matthew might not like to hear about what everyone assumed to be a colorful, exciting, scandalous love life. It was anything but. It was depressing, painful, humiliating. None of the women who were openly jealous of the attention she got from men suspected she would give twenty years of her life to be left alone. None of the people who condemned her for her supposed eagerness to be bedded stopped to wonder whether it was what she truly wanted. And, of course, none of the men who took advantage of it bothered to check if she was willing—they simply took her agreement as a given.

No one knew, or would believe, that she never encouraged men, never sought them out, never took the first step.

Except with Matthew.

Why him? For the thousandth time, she asked herself that question. He seemed an unlikely choice. Not only was he English, but he was hostile to the Welsh as well, to everything she loved, and he hated everything she represented. He'd been fiercely opposed to Connor's marriage to Esyllt last year, going as far as hiding from his brother the role she had played in his rescue from the Welsh rebels who had abducted him. This had caused a rift between husband and wife, a rift which had mercifully been bridged since then. But it went to show that the man could be ruthlessness personified with people he didn't approve of.

Admittedly, he had overcome his prejudice and come to his senses where Esyllt was concerned. He was now a reliable ally to her, as well as a loving, attentive uncle to her daughter by her first marriage, Siân.

Still.

He should be the last man Branwen should be drawn to. Pity he was also the first.

"What are those sweets made of?" she asked, plucking another almond from the silver dish, indicating that the topic of Matthew and why she had kissed him was closed.

"Good, are they not?" Esyllt sighed as she sat back in her chair, one hand over her swollen belly. "They are dusted in cinnamon, a spice brought from the Holy Land. Connor tasted them when he visited court some years ago, and he remembered them when I told him about my craving for all things sweet. He thought they might please me, and never have I had more cause to congratulate myself on being his wife, because it was just what I needed."

Branwen afforded a smile. They both knew that his willingness to procure treats for his wife was the least of Connor's qualities.

"What does this cinnamon look like?" She had never heard of it.

"It's actually the bark of a tree. It comes in long curls that can be steeped into stews or it can be reduced to a rich, fragrant powder the color of chestnuts that can be used as salt." Esyllt popped a sweet into her mouth and sighed in contentment. "Incredible, is it not? Who would have thought of flavoring anything with tree bark? I, in any case, have never tasted anything like it."

Branwen nodded in agreement, but she had already tasted it.

On Matthew Hunter's tongue.

∼

"Come, you lazy sod, is that the best you can do?" Matthew taunted, lowering his sword. He was torn between amusement and exasperation. "Are you fighting me or falling asleep? Where's your legendary stamina? I swear you've grown soft since we left England, Lord Sheridan! You didn't spend your days yawning then, and you could hold your own against me."

Clasping him by the forearm, he helped his brother up.

"I didn't spend half the night awake then, that's why," Connor grinned, not in the least chastened. "Now, with Esyllt, it's different. I'm most definitely ... *up* most of the night. No wonder I can barely stand when you summon me at dawn. But I am telling you, there is nothing wrong with my stamina, and I don't see how I will ever grow soft, considering all the energy I expend in my marital bed."

"You really are an animal, rutting all night with your wife in her condition." Matthew scoffed, though he was secretly jealous of his brother's matrimonial bliss. His marriage to the beautiful and loving Welsh woman had been the making of him. His first union had not been a love match, and the difference was glaring. Connor was now a happy man and it showed. "You are aware she is heavy with child, are you not?"

"Very aware, as I am the one responsible for this wonderful state of affairs." A shadow passed over his brother's face, removing all traces of his smile. "You don't think my attentions could damage Esyllt or the babe, do you? Perhaps you're right. Perhaps I've been too demanding. Should I refrain from touching her until the birth?"

Though he knew full well why Connor would worry about this, having already lost two children, Matthew could not help another scoff.

"I think that if you denied her your touch, your little wife would hunt you down after two days to demand you resume your 'attentions', as you call them, without delay. She likes them well enough, from what I can hear."

The provocation had the desired effect. Connor's eyes flashed. All of a sudden, he was wide awake and ready to fight. "You dare listen to us?"

"Not 'listen', exactly, but a man has ears, in case you didn't know."

Connor lifted his sword. Good. Another well-aimed taunt and he might actually start using it. After more than three days without training, Matthew was raring to go, and his brother was the only one who could give him what he needed. No one else at Esgyrn Castle could match him in speed and skill—when he was awake, that was.

If he had to needle him to restore him to his usual state, then so be it. Why should Esyllt be the only one to benefit from the man's stamina?

"I can't help but hear her sweet little moans," he said, making sure to waggle his brows. "And I will admit the sound rather inflames the imagination. Your boar-like grunting, though, I could do without. It's rather distract—"

Before he could finish the sentence, Connor lunged at him. The exchange that ensued was one of the fiercest they'd ever had and, despite the chilly temperature in the bailey, they were both sweating by the time Matthew's sword flew out of his hand to land fifteen yards to his right.

A smile tugged at his lips. Well. He'd wanted his brother at his best, and he'd certainly gotten it.

"Listen to me, you cur, you are either moving rooms today," Connor warned, placing the tip of his sword against Matthew's neck to force his chin up, "or tomorrow, I cut off your ears. Is that understood?"

"Calm down, Con, I was jesting. If I could hear anything, believe me, I would have moved long ago."

Indeed. For a celibate man, or as near as, being subjected to such provocative sounds while he lay alone in bed would be much akin to torture. His nights had been hard enough of late. No matter what, he didn't seem able to get a certain dark-haired Welsh woman out of his head, and more than once he'd relived their passionate kiss while he fisted himself to bring about a release that never seemed to satisfy him. It was the first time he had obsessed about a woman thus and he didn't like it one little bit.

Why her? True, their kiss had been breathtaking, but kisses were not meant to be life-changing events, were they? It had certainly never been the case before. He wasn't even sure when, or if, he would see Branwen again. Perhaps he could find a pretext for Esyllt to invite her to the castle? The two of them seemed close, even though they came from very different backgrounds.

The pressure under his chin eased, allowing him to breathe again. Not that he'd worried Connor would actually cut him. He'd never been in any real danger, but all the same, he preferred not to have a blade pressed against his throat.

Because he knew he had nothing to fear, he could not resist one last provocation.

"If you do not want anyone to hear your little wife moan, then I suggest you stop taking her in every dark corner you can find."

Had Matthew not ducked in time, he would have found himself on the receiving end of Connor's sword hilt. As, thankfully, his reflexes were as good as they'd ever been, the hard metal hit the stone wall instead of his skull.

He waited, a smile floating on his lips, while his brother mastered his temper once more.

"Aye, perhaps I should do that," Connor said at last. "If only she weren't so bloody alluring, it might help me keep a cool head."

Matthew was about to point out that the head was not the part of him that needed to remain cool, then thought it wiser to hold his tongue this time. He had no intention of ending up with an injury when he pushed his brother too far. He would not be killed, but he might well end up with a broken limb. The pain and inconvenience that would ensue were not worth the satisfaction of rankling Connor, who appeared genuinely worried.

"I'm glad to see you so content," he said instead. "I know your marriage to Helen was not a happy one, and Esyllt is the perfect woman for you."

"That she is." Connor nodded, finally restored to his usual

composure. "Having a loving wife is a blessing indeed." He paused, then sheathed his sword back in his scabbard. "What about you?"

"What about me?" Matthew pretended not to have understood the question.

"You've just turned thirty. Are you ever going to consider marrying? If what Jane and Siân told us the other day is true, then it—"

Everything within him tightened. His brother knew about the kiss with Branwen? Damn it all, he should have made the little girls swear to secrecy. Next time he would be sure to catch them by the scruff of the neck and make them promise not to say anything to anyone. He blinked when the thought hit him.

Next time?

Did he really expect there would be a next time? No, it was even worse than that, he realized with a sinking feeling. He wasn't expecting it, he was *hoping* for it.

"You have taken up gossiping then, like an old woman?" he snarled, snatching his sword from the ground. "Fie, what has become of the mighty warrior you once were?"

Connor was not so easily riled this time, since the conversation was not centered around his wife. He merely shrugged. "It's not gossiping if it's true. In all our lives, I have never seen or even *heard* of you kissing anyone, much less in such a public place. This has to mean something, hence my question."

Yes, it most probably meant something, but Matthew was not sure what yet. He'd been trying to puzzle it out for days, in vain. All he knew was that he had been surprised, because for the first time in his life, a woman had kissed him, not the other way around. He'd wanted to kiss Branwen, admittedly, but she had placed her lips on his before he could make the decision to do so. The thrill her boldness had provoked inside him had been like nothing else, and the ensuing kiss had been spectacular.

But that woman was the last who should provoke anything inside him because it could spell danger.

She was Welsh, and he knew all too well what the Welsh thought of the English, whom they saw as oppressors they should rid themselves of. He also knew the length some of them were prepared to go to get to their enemies. The rebels weren't above using women as pawns in their game of domination. Only a few months ago, Connor had almost died when a Welshman had forced his wife to hand him over to men who tortured him and would have killed him had Matthew not reached him in time. Poor Esyllt had had no choice but to do the bastard's bidding, for fear of never seeing her daughter again.

Was Gruffydd, who had escaped punishment the day Matthew had rescued Connor, even now plotting his revenge against the new masters of Esgyrn Castle and using Branwen as a tool to get to them? Or was it someone else, one of his vile friends who meant to make him pay for his role in rescuing Lord Sheridan from the fate planned for him? Had they decided to send the beautiful woman to him, hoping to catch him unawares because he would be too busy thinking with his cock to use his head in her presence? The risk was very real, because they had chosen their weapon well.

The dark-haired, golden-eyed, straight-speaking beauty drew him like no one else ever had.

Regardless, he could not afford to feel anything other than suspicion toward a woman who had thrown herself into his arms upon first acquaintance as if it were the normal thing to do. First, he had to find out who this Branwen was, and who, if anyone, had sent her to lure him into danger.

Then and only then would he be free to explore the feelings she stirred in him. If they had not disappeared in the meantime, of course. He still wasn't convinced this was any more than a pathetic infatuation brought on by too many years denying himself what he wanted.

"Enough blabbering!" Matthew snapped, cutting the air with his sword. It would be his turn to make his brother regret his taunts. *"En garde.* Now that you've finally woken up, let us stop playing."

Chapter Two

The landscape was beautiful seen from so high. Branwen stared through the open bay window, fascinated. No matter how many times she had come to the castle, the view from the top never failed to amaze her. It was even more spectacular from the battlements, of course, but today's weather precluded a long stay outside. Much better to observe it from the comfort of the solar.

Over the years, since her friend Esyllt had come to live at Castell Esgyrn with her first husband, she'd had the chance to see her native hills in every season, like a precious carpet unfolding at her feet. Vibrant with mint-green leaves in the spring, lush and brimming with wildlife in the summer, dazzling wrapped in rich colors in the fall. Right now, frozen into immobility by winter's icy fingers, they weren't any less beautiful, if in a haunting way. The skeletal trees were spread like lace over the pale blue sky.

Just as she was wondering how long they would have to wait for the first flowers to burst through the barren ground, movement to her left caught her eye. A small retinue on horseback, perhaps a dozen strong, was approaching from the east, having just crested the nearest hill.

Branwen turned to Esyllt, who, sitting by the brazier, wouldn't have seen anything.

"Someone is coming," she informed her, doing her best to keep the worry from her voice. People coming from the east could all too easily be coming from England, and that was rarely good news. It did not look like a huge, invading army led by King Edward himself, but you never knew.

Her friend joined her by the window, and frowned when she saw whence the horses had come. She would have reached the same conclusion as Branwen. These could be scouts sent ahead of a larger contingent, exactly what every Welsh person feared. She fell rather than sat on the stone bench behind her.

"Connor is not in the castle at present. I think I had better wait here until we know who the riders are, and let Master William deal with them," Esyllt said, eyeing her swollen stomach. There was no mistaking her meaning. At the best of times, her husband would not want her to confront a dozen aggressive Englishmen on her own. Right now, heavy with his child, she was not to place herself in any danger whatsoever.

Branwen could only agree. You never knew where you stood with the arrogant invaders, or rather, you knew it all too well. In a position of inferiority. It was better not to play with fire.

"Let us stay here and see what transpires," she suggested.

Huddled together by the window, Esyllt and Branwen waited anxiously. Soon enough, ten horses rode through the gate in a clatter of hooves. From their vantage point of view, the two women could see them clearly. A young man was riding at the head of the group, clearly in charge of the expedition.

"'Tis only Connor's cousins George and Elena," Esyllt declared, sounding relieved. "I didn't dare hope as much, since we were expecting them later this week. All is well."

Branwen allowed herself to relax. Danger was averted, and she should not have allowed herself to get riled up so easily.

"Shall we go and greet them?" she asked, smiling to her friend.

"Yes. Would you go get Connor for me, tell him they've arrived? He's gone to the lake for a swim." Esyllt placed a hand on her stomach and stroked it tenderly. "I'm afraid I can barely muster the strength to go to the bailey, never mind make it down the hill and back."

"Of course," Branwen soothed. Her friend looked exhausted. It was not hard to guess she had difficulty sleeping at night, being so close to her term. Of course, Branwen herself had never been with child, but she imagined it took its toll on a woman's body. "You stay here, I will be but a moment."

Esyllt sighed in relief. "Thank you. Meanwhile, I will go welcome George and Elena."

Wrapping herself in her cloak, Branwen took the path that descended to the lake. The timid sun overhead was not enough to heat her back and she shivered. A swim in this weather, she mused, was the man mad? The water would be icy cold. What on earth could have possessed Connor to even attempt it? It just went to show that not all Englishmen were pampered weaklings, not fit to live the life of a Welshman, as she often heard the villagers say. Of course, to her, Englishmen were more like entitled lechers, who took what they wanted how they wanted it, especially women.

But Connor Hunter was not like that. He was as good a man as she had ever met.

She was glad for her friend, who had found happiness with her second husband. Gwyn had been a good man, but Esyllt had not been in love with him. Now, she was most definitely in love, and no one could doubt Connor, English as he may be, returned her feelings. The two of them only had eyes for one another. The kind of marriage they had would make anyone jealous, even someone like her, who thought a perfect life would be one free of men.

To ward off the cold seeping into her bones, Branwen increased the speed of her walk, and soon, the lake was in view. As she rounded the bend, all the air left her lungs.

Oh, Connor was at the lake, as she'd expected. He had indeed gone for a swim. Only, Esyllt had forgotten to mention that he was not alone, but with his brother, and that both men would be gloriously, shockingly, jaw-droppingly naked. Frozen to the spot, she watched them walk out of the water, revealing their chiseled warrior bodies inch by inch, until they stood with only their feet in the water.

The air around her stilled. Suddenly she didn't feel the cold, or even her own body.

Avert your eyes. Run away. Warn them of your presence. Do something! her mind urged.

She didn't look away, she stayed where she was, she was careful not to betray her presence in any way, and she did absolutely nothing, save for staring at the men in front of her. Guilt caused heat to burn her cheeks. What would Esyllt say if she knew her friend seen her husband naked? Then she realized that she had barely spared a glance to Connor, instead focusing on the blond man to his right.

Branwen had seen more men naked or bare-chested than she cared to remember or had wished to, but none of them could compare with Matthew. Up until then, she would not have thought that the simple fact of seeing a man's chest could make her body heat in desire, but unquestionably, it did.

He had long, elegant arms that not only were perfectly sculpted, but were adorned with veins that coursed all the way down from his rounded shoulders to his beautiful hands. A smattering of hairs that were as shiny as gold drew the eye to his pectorals and down a stomach that appeared to be hewn of polished stone. And of course ...

Don't look, do not look.

But she did more than look. She drank in every inch of his perfect shape, already knowing that the image would haunt her for years to come. They had kissed the previous week and the notion had bewildered her for days. Why had she felt the impulse to kiss this man? She had tried to tell herself that there was more to it than pure physical attraction. True, he was handsome, but she had seen other men who could lay claim to that title. She had not been interested in the least.

But now ... now she was most decidedly interested. The urge to kiss Matthew again bloomed inside her. Because he was not just handsome, he was worryingly, almost unnaturally alluring. A blond pagan god. Having seen him in his naked glory, she could not ignore it any longer.

She'd kissed him because she wanted him.

A squirrel jumped from a tree and the noise caused the men to swivel around—and look straight at her. For a moment, no one moved.

Then the squirrel scuttered away, shaking them all out of their immobility.

"Branwen!" Connor snatched his tunic from the ground and held it protectively in front of his manhood. Matthew, she noticed, was in less of a hurry to cover himself up, as if he wanted to taunt her with the proof of his virility. The look in his eyes made it clear he would not have bothered with trying to preserve his modesty if they had been alone.

You're welcome to look your fill, it seemed to say. *I know you like what you see.*

"Forgive us, we had no idea someone would be walking by. Would you mind turning around while we make ourselves decent?" Connor asked, glaring at his brother as if to ask what he was playing at by just standing there.

"Of course not," Branwen mumbled, thinking that she should have done so of her own accord long ago.

She heard the rustle of clothes and tried very hard not to imagine muscles bulging and arms flexing when the men struggled to get their wet bodies into their clothes. There was some muttering, then Connor called out. "Thank you. You can turn around."

He was fully dressed, whereas Matthew had only put on his braies, which hung low on his hips, revealing more than they hid, drawing the eye to the stomach she had admired just before. She guessed the muttering had been Connor admonishing him for not covering up more. She should have been offended, but she was too fascinated to mind. No one should cover up such beauty.

"Did you want something?" Connor asked, his voice slightly huskier than usual.

With some effort, she remembered why she was here. "No, but Esyllt s-sent me to get you," she stammered. "To tell you your—"

"What's wrong? Is it the babe?" he instantly asked, worry making him pale. Silly her. She had worried him with her hesitation.

"No, she's perfectly all right. There's nothing wrong with her or the babe." Branwen smiled reassuringly, knowing why he would worry more than the average man about the notion of his wife going into labor. Her friend had confided in her about the tragic losses her husband had suffered shortly before his arrival to Wales. His first wife had died in childbed, along with the babe she was carrying. As if that was not enough, a few weeks later he had lost his daughter Jane's twin sister. As a result, he dreaded the moment Esyllt would have to give birth. "'Tis only that your cousins George and Elena have arrived."

His shoulders sagged in relief. "Already? But we didn't expect them before the end of the week."

"So Esyllt said, but apparently they are here. She sent me to get you because she could not muster the courage to come all the way to the lake herself."

Once again it appeared she had said the wrong thing. Connor tensed up again, as if he thought she was hiding the true state of affairs from him. Branwen mentally kicked herself. Why did she have to mention Esyllt's fatigue?

"I'll go," he snapped. "Matthew, you'll meet us in the great hall when you're decent, and not a moment sooner, do you hear?"

Not even throwing one glance at his brother, he set off at a run in the direction of the castle—and Branwen was left alone with Matthew.

Matthew, who made a point of remaining bare-chested and was staring at her with a half-smile on his lips. His full, beautiful, sinful lips. The lips she had kissed, and wanted to kiss still. What was wrong with her? She had never been attracted to a man thus, never even thought it could happen to her. If it had to happen to her, couldn't she at least choose a man she could consider taking as a lover? Someone not so above herself, not so infuriatingly arrogant, not so English?

"You've been avoiding me."

It wasn't a question, but a statement of fact, and though they both knew why that might be, Branwen pretended not to know what he was referring to. "I haven't. Why would I?"

"You have," he snapped, not in the least impressed. "And I'm not in the habit of allowing people to ignore me, much less people I've kissed."

"'People'? Interesting choice of words. Don't you mean 'women'?" she challenged.

The glare he threw her would have curdled milk. How could such warm-colored eyes appear so cold, she wondered? Connor, despite the icy hue of his green eyes, never gave her the impression her marrow had frozen in her bones when he looked at her. Really, the two brothers were like night and day, which was little wonder when one considered they were not really brothers at all, at least not related by blood.

"If you mean to avoid giving me an explanation by provoking my anger, you'd better think again. Suggesting that I go around kissing men is not going to make me forget that I'm still waiting for you to justify your behavior," he barked. "You had better tell me right now what you mean by kissing me one day, then vanishing into thin air the next."

There was a pause. Then finally, she answered. And the manner in which she did took her by surprise. She'd meant to tease him, not be so honest, but her mouth had other ideas.

"I don't usually go around kissing men."

Not in the least impressed by what had been a very private admission, Matthew snorted. "No, that I can well believe."

Then you'd be the only one, Branwen thought ruefully. But although no one would believe her, and she had been bedded by more men than she could count, this was no lie. She'd never kissed a man of her own volition before. She usually went out of her way to avoid men, and every kiss she'd ever experienced had been imposed on her.

"It scared me. I could not make sense of the urge to kiss you and it scared me. That's why I fled."

There it was. The stark, complete truth. It had cost her every ounce of courage to utter it, but she needed to make him understand. Perhaps it would help her to understand. What would he do with her confession? To her dismay, he scoffed again.

"I see. The little virgin bit off more than she could chew?"

Little virgin.

The two words were a punch to the gut. How wrong he was! If only she were untouched ...

"I am no virgin," she whispered.

As soon as the words left her mouth, Branwen regretted them. No doubt Matthew would use the unexpected confession to mock her further. She could tell it had startled him, but as could have been expected from such a confident man, he recovered quickly. A slow smile curved his lips.

"Well then, if you're not a virgin, a mere kiss could not have frightened you. You've been through much worse."

She blinked. He'd chosen to tease her rather than use her admission against her, for which she was oddly grateful. She would have hated to hear him call her a whore.

"It did because, as I told you, I don't usually go around kissing men. I don't understand what happened to me."

What was pushing her to insist? Why did she feel the urge to be so honest, especially in front of his refusal to see the confession for what it was, a breakthrough moment for her?

"I will tell you what happened to you, then, shall I?" Matthew purred. "It's not so difficult to understand. You wanted me. What's more, you still do. You can't see the way you look at my body, but I can. Your eyes are glowing. You want me. It's the only explanation."

He was making light of it, but Matthew was surprised by the desire he could see in Branwen's eyes when she looked at him, because he was still convinced she had been sent by Gruffydd or another Welsh rebel to get to him. It was not a bad strategy, he had to admit. A woman as beautiful as she was could make any man lose his head. But what Gruffydd, along with everyone else, didn't know was that he had a lifetime of control to draw from. He'd become a master of restraint, and it would take more than a pretty face to make him throw caution to the wind. Even if that face was adorned with glowing golden eyes.

Before he did anything, he had to know who had sent her. His life, and perhaps even that of Connor's family, might depend on it. He could not allow his senses to overrule his reason.

"Am I to believe you wanted me so much that you just kissed me, even though you claim you don't usually do that, even though I barely know your name?"

"It's Branwen," she reminded him unnecessarily. He had not forgotten it. "It means white raven."

Matthew gave out a laugh. Why had she added that piece of information? He had no idea, but he was delighted with it. "Of course. We all know ravens are white. And what does Esyllt mean then? Cold sun, bitter honey? Really, why can't you Welsh people choose sensible names?"

"Like Matthew you mean?" she replied, visibly piqued.

"Exactly like Matthew."

She pursed her pretty lips, not in the least beaten. "Let me think. Matthew the apostle was a tax collector, was he not? Very sensible. One might even say ... uninspiring."

So the woman wanted to tease him back? Two could play at this game. Matthew smiled inwardly. This might be the opportunity he'd needed to find out more about her and her motives for wanting to be with him. Here, alone, away from prying eyes and ears, he might get some information out of her.

"If you find me uninspiring, why did you kiss me the other day?" He took a step toward her and whispered, "You could have waited for me to kiss you. That is what women usually do, especially the ones who claim not to be used to pouncing on men. I think there must be something about me you must find inspiring, whatever you say."

Her reaction pleased him. He had unnerved her.

"I-I said your *name* was uninspiring, not you," she stammered. He took another step forward.

"Ah. A crucial distinction. But please answer my question. Why did you kiss me? Or rather, who demanded that you got near me?"

"What do you mean, 'demanded'? No one demanded anything. We were alone in the solar."

She appeared genuinely confused by the question. Either she was very good at lying or she was innocent of all scheming. He would have to be more direct, and see how she reacted.

"Was it Gruffydd?"

Her eyes widened, allowing the extraordinary color of the irises to pierce through him like a golden arrow. "Gruffydd ap Hywel? The man who almost killed Connor? You mean you know where he's hiding?" She brought both her hands to her chest. "Oh, that is good news, for he should pay for what he did to them!"

This was such a heartfelt answer that he knew without a doubt Gruffydd was not the one using her.

"No. I don't know where the man is hiding."

Her face fell in disappointment, and he felt a pang of regret for having caused her momentary hope to avenge her friend's family. Then she frowned, visibly nonplussed. "Why did you mention him then? I'm not sure I'm following you."

"No. Evidently, you're not." And he would gain nothing by carrying on this interrogation.

"I would like to return to the castle, if I may," Branwen said, wrapping her cloak more tightly around herself. Whether she was cold or merely trying to protect herself from the discomfort his proximity was provoking was not certain. He smirked. Whatever it was, it was clear she was unsettled.

"What's the hurry?"

She didn't answer but he already knew the answer to that question.

Nothing. But I need to escape you in all your naked glory.

There was no way she would admit to this out loud of course, so she simply turned around and headed for the castle.

Matthew watched her go pensively. He'd made no progress in discovering who had sent her to him. Even more puzzling, he now had the impression that no one had. Not only had she seemed confused by his questions, rather than caught out, but the way she had looked at his body had betrayed genuine admiration.

He was starting to think no one had made her kiss him, and that only the desire a woman felt in front of a man she found appealing was responsible for the urge. She might well be telling the truth about that at least. Which only added to the draw she had on him. If she was here of her own volition, then there was no reason for him to resist the attraction. Because attracted he was. And intrigued, more than ever.

He ran after her, unable to be parted from her just yet. "Wait. There's something I wanted to ask you."

Branwen's heart plummeted. This would be about their kiss again, she could feel it in her bones. Matthew would demand she explained why she had kissed him if, as she'd claimed, she didn't go around kissing men. But she had told him all she could tell him on the subject, and he had not believed her. Could she perhaps make him—

"Where did they find the skeletons exactly?"

She blinked. The skeletons. What skeletons? She had been so sure he would want to embarrass her by alluding to their kiss that it took her a moment to understand he was talking about something else. "What are you talking about?"

"Connor and Esyllt told me Esgyrn Castle meant Bones Castle, and this because when they dug the ditches for the foundations, they found two skeletons lying there. So I was wondering where they'd been found exactly. You will know."

"I don't. The castle is over a hundred years old, in case you hadn't noticed," she answered, more testily than she had intended. "I wasn't born yet when it was built."

The laugh he gave resonated all the way down her body. It was a rich, joyous laugh, completely at odds with his brooding persona. If she didn't know better, she would have said that a man who laughed like this could not pose any danger to anyone.

"Worry not, I wasn't for a moment suggesting you were a day over sixty."

"Sixty!" She almost choked on the word. "I'm seven-and-twenty!"

His brown eyes twinkled. When they were not cold with disdain, they were as warm as the spice powder coating the almonds Esyllt had given her the other day. Cinnamon. It was that warmth which made her understand he'd only been teasing her. Of course, he had. Who in their right mind would think her a woman in her old age? She really was a ninny where he was concerned.

"The skeletons were found just over there." She indicated a place to their left, at random. In truth, she had no idea where the remains had been found, but she had a feeling he would not let her go before she'd given him an answer. "I suspect they were a couple of arrogant Englishmen who should have stayed in their country and who froze to death after bathing in the lake in the middle of winter and forgot to get dressed afterward. I have seen it happen. It seems that some people will never learn."

With those words, she turned on her heels.

Matthew's rich laugh chased after her all the way up the hill.

～

When he set off toward the castle some time later, Matthew was shivering. Damn it all, he'd not been cold while talking to Branwen, quite the opposite, but even so, he should not have remained bare-chested after his bath. Though he had now put his shirt and tunic back on, he didn't seem able to shake the cold wrapping around his bones. His lips curled when he remembered Branwen teasing him about ending up like the two skeletons in the ditch, dead from the cold. The woman was fearless. Shouldn't she be wary of angering him when alone with him? Yes. And instead, she took pleasure in provoking him.

But despite her infuriating ways, the only thing she stirred in him when she tried to be contrary was his lust, which was not the wisest reaction. He should be on his guard when alone with her, not trying to imagine excuses to draw her into his arms. Undoubtedly, it would be the foolish thing to do, because if she had indeed been sent to him by an enemy, then she was most probably armed. Should he check the next time they met? Run his fingers down her arms, up her back, and along her slender thighs?

Matthew cursed out loud because all the question had managed to do was make him undress her mentally to try and decide where she might be hiding her weapon. Was she carrying a blade hidden in her bodice? Did she have a knife strapped to her thigh, its pointy end pressing into her tender flesh, ever so close to her woman's secret? The thought made him shiver, a bad idea when he was already too cold for comfort. There was only one thing to do.

Break into a run, and stop only when his blood had cooled

and the rest of his body had warmed up. It took longer than he had hoped to achieve this result, and by the time he passed through the gate, he was sweating. As if to mock his efforts, the first person he saw in the bailey was none other than Branwen.

He planted himself in front of her, unable to do the sensible thing and walk away.

"Kindly let me pass. I was on my way back home," she said, wrapping her cloak more securely around herself. It could have been because she was cold, of course, but just like before, he had the impression she was doing so to control the impulse to throw herself into his arms.

The thought pleased him, until he remembered she would only do that to get to him and plunge the dagger she was hiding into his gut.

"Setting off on foot? You don't have a mount then?" There was no need for her to answer, as he had not seen any unknown horse tethered by the stables. He'd already guessed she would be walking. "And where is 'home', exactly?" The more he knew about her, the better.

"In the village down the valley." She cocked her head. "Why are you even asking? Did you think I was a grand lady, living in my own castle?"

"No."

That she was not a noble or even a rich woman was clear. Her clothes were plain and serviceable, her manners vastly different from Esyllt's. A thought suddenly struck him. Connor had told him that the two women had known one another almost all their lives. If that were true, it made the possibility of her having been sent to Esgyrn Castle to get to him less plausible. A friend of his sister-in-law's would surely not want to hurt her husband's brother.

Unless of course, that elusive someone had blackmailed her into doing his bidding. Last year Gruffydd had forced Esyllt to hand Connor over to his mob of bloodthirsty men in exchange for her young daughter's life. Was it not possible another Welsh rebel had seized on Branwen's proximity to the lady of the castle to get to him? Yes. All too possible.

He let out a grunt of frustration. Why was it so complicated? Why could he not simply act on the attraction he felt toward her without worrying about her ulterior motive? In England, things had been much simpler where women were concerned. He'd never worried about what they wanted from him. It had been clear enough. Not for the first time he wished he could return home, away from plotting men and vexing, golden-eyed beauties.

"I was wondering whether you—"

A series of shrieks interrupted him. Then a woman's voice reached them from the other side of the barbican. She was talking in English.

"Let me go, you big oaf! I don't want you to touch me!"

"I'll touch you if I want to. What are you going to do about it?"

Elena and George, fighting as usual. Matthew would have recognized their voices anywhere. He rolled his eyes. They had only just arrived, could they not leave be for a day? Branwen looked at him in horror when the protests continued. Evidently, she was worried for the woman she thought was being assaulted. Before he could explain that it was not a real attack, only his cousins being their usual, silly selves, she rushed in the direction of the noise.

He ran after her. "Wait, it's not what you think, there's no need to intervene."

But she ignored him and, a moment later, fell on George's back. As soon as she landed on him, she started to pummel him. Matthew could not help a laugh at the shock on the youth's face. The little hellion had misread the scene and thought she was coming to Elena's rescue, and after all, why would he not let her help the girl? George was a year older and stronger than his sister, why should he always have the upper hand? It would do him good to be brought to heel for once.

He crossed his arms over his chest to see how the lad would handle the assault, but soon the laughter died in his throat. If he didn't stop her, Branwen might well inflict some serious damage on his cousin. Oblivious to his protests, she was hitting him wherever she could get purchase, screaming in Welsh all the while.

The commotion was such that it soon brought Connor and Esyllt running.

"What's going on here?" his brother asked, taking in the scene in one glance.

"Help!" George cried. To his credit, the boy was not defending himself as he would have against a male opponent. He would easily have been able to rid himself of Branwen if he'd put his heart in it, but he seemed loath to risk hurting her. Matthew could only admire him for it. It was what decided him. He could not let the poor lad get ripped to shreds in front of his eyes because he was being gallant. It had lasted long enough.

He reached out to Branwen, but she hit him hard on the side of the face as soon as he put his hand on her. Stars blurred his vision and his respect for George increased tenfold. It would not be as easy as he had imagined to bring her to heel.

"Ow, easy, woman!" he growled. "Or I'll have no choice but to stun you."

She didn't appear to understand, or even hear the command. It seemed to him she was repeating the same thing over and over again. He wasn't even sure she was addressing him, as she was speaking in Welsh. Struggling to stop her from swinging her arms, he turned to Esyllt.

"What is she saying?"

"Leave her alone, she's just a child," his sister-in-law translated, a frown on her face. "Leave her be, again and again."

Damnation, she had really taken the defense of Elena to heart.

"It's all right," Connor joined in, talking to Branwen in soothing tones. "Elena and George are just messing around. They often do that."

The reassurance didn't have any effect, and Esyllt repeated the words in Welsh. Eventually, spent by the fierce fight, Branwen stopped struggling. She looked at Matthew, eyes dazed, for a brief moment—and fainted clean away. Only the fact that he was still holding her prevented her from falling flat on her face.

He swept her up in his arms before he could topple over to the ground with her.

"What the hell was that about?" he whispered, looking at the unconscious woman in his arms. Never had he witnessed a more unlikely scene.

"I have no idea." Connor appeared just as nonplussed.

Esyllt was not so easily impressed. "Bring her to my bed," she instructed, already heading that way. "I will take care of her."

∽

"I brought you some sugared almonds. I think it might do you good to eat something."

"Thank you." Branwen didn't take one or even open her eyes. Not only was her head still spinning but she wasn't sure she could face being with anyone right now, even her dearest friend. There was an odd taste in her mouth and a weight crushing her chest.

At first, upon waking up, she had wondered what she was

doing in a comfortable bed, but then everything had come back to her in a rush. The fight. Her powerlessness.

Matthew holding her tight against him.

"You want to tell me why the sight of George and Elena fighting affected you so much?" Esyllt asked gently. Branwen guessed from the way she was holding her hand that her friend was sitting next to her on the edge of the bed.

She kept her eyes closed and thought. Did she want to explain what had happened?

She wasn't sure. If she said it out loud, there would be no pretending it wasn't real anymore. Not that she had any doubt about it.

There was a pause, then Esyllt spoke again. "I think it has to do with something you've never dared to share with me, something that makes your life unbearable."

Unbearable. Yes, that was exactly what it was. Unbearable.

Branwen opened her eyes. The worry and concern she saw in her friend's eyes decided her. Perhaps it was time to confide in someone. Instinct told her she wouldn't be judged.

"I'm not who you think I am, what everyone thinks I am," she started slowly. "I'm not this carefree, wanton woman who beds all the men she wants for her pleasure."

I'm a trapped woman who cannot escape the men who want to bed her for their pleasure.

"No. This much I had suspected," her friend said cautiously. "For all your supposed conquests, you have never mentioned a single man to me, and you always go out of your way not to find yourself alone with men. This is not the behavior of a carefree, wanton woman, if you ask me."

No, it wasn't.

"When I was fifteen summers, an important local lord came to visit the village. He found me alone in the clearing."

A heavy silence followed. Then, somehow, under Esyllt's

compassionate gaze, Branwen managed to tell the whole horrific story, leaving no details out.

"When I saw George wrestling Elena, who must be the age I was then, I just ... somehow it brought it all back. She screamed that she didn't want to be touched and it tore at my guts. I couldn't bear it. I'm sorry."

"Don't be sorry!" There was a pause. "My God, Branwen, I had my suspicions regarding your past, but this is so much worse than I imagined." Esyllt shook her head then something flashed in her eyes. Hatred. Determination. "This man should be punished for what he did. Tell me who he is and where we can find him so we—"

"No!" Branwen sat bolt upright in the bed, panic blooming in her chest. "It will be useless. He's too powerful, no one will dare stand up to him, and what's worse, he's well-liked, from what I can gather. I'm nobody. No one will believe me, and this would be worse than everything else." After what she had endured, she could not bear to have people dismiss her claim or accuse her of lying.

"*I* believe you!" Esyllt stood up, her whole body radiating outrage.

"Yes, so I see, and I thank you for it, but you're a woman, and my friend."

"Connor is a man, and I'm sure he will—"

"No! I would rather you didn't tell him anything. I could not bear it."

Oh, what had she done? She should never have opened up.

"Very well, I'll not tell him," her friend said reluctantly. "But we will find out who this man is, and make him pay one way or the other, you mark my word. I am lady of this castle, and my husband is a powerful lord in his own right, and well-liked as well. He will see to it that the man is punished."

"Please, Esyllt. I'm grateful for your support but I cannot suffer it right now. I just want to go home."

"Home! You're in no state to go anywhere. You will stay here tonight, and that's final. I will not hear any different."

Esyllt rarely acted the mighty lady with her, or indeed anyone, but tonight Branwen was grateful for her high-handedness, because after reliving the nightmare of the assault, the last thing she wanted was to be on her own. She would never have dared ask to stay the night at Castell Esgyrn, but it was exactly what she needed.

"Thank you." She gave her friend's hand a squeeze. "Now, I would like a moment alone, if I may."

"Of course."

Alone at last, Branwen reached out for a sugared almond—and burst into tears when Matthew's taste, so warm and spicy, hit her tongue.

Oh, she was in deep trouble.

Chapter Three

"Who do you really think it was, then?"

Branwen let out a whelp when a deep voice sliced through the silence of the solar. She had taken refuge there after having gone to see Elena and George to apologize for her behavior the previous day, and had been engrossed in the spectacle playing out through the window. Down below, in the field beyond the lists, two hares were fighting, their stances slightly ridiculous even though they were bursting with aggressivity. She could not help but feel that she might have looked like that when she had pounced on George, both violent and ludicrous.

"Did you really have to do that, English?" she snapped, turning to face Matthew. She was so annoyed that the insulting word slipped right out of her mouth. "You scared the life out of me."

The wretched man walked forward, a smile floating on his lips. As could have been predicted, he was not impressed by the rebuke. "You shouldn't get so engrossed in what you're doing if you don't want people to take you by surprise. You should always be on your guard."

Oh, she usually was. In fact, she spent her life watching out for potential trouble. It was exhausting. But here, inside Castell Esgyrn, she'd thought herself safe.

Knowing Matthew would enjoy seeing he had riled her, she repressed a scoff. It was not her fault she had been startled, but his. He had done it on purpose. He would have guessed from the way she was examining the landscape that she was not paying attention to what was happening behind her. And that was another thing. How long had he watched her, unnoticed? The thought of his gaze roving over her made her blood heat up, when usually being the object of male attention froze the marrow in her bones.

"*Other people* should have had the decency to let their presence be known when they enter a room, so as not to startle anyone," she pointed out, lifting her chin.

"Mm, yes, you mean like you did at the lake yesterday. Have the decency to let your presence be known." Matthew had the audacity to smile. "I think Connor and I owe that squirrel a debt of gratitude. Had he not decided to leap from one tree to the next, I think you would have ogled us until we finally decided to get dressed. Not that I minded."

The heat that had started on her cheeks spread to her chest. The odious man! Of course, he'd guessed she had spent a long time admiring—ogling, as he'd said—his naked form, and he was taking delight in telling her as much. He crossed his arms over his chest, and she wondered if he was not doing it to draw attention to his bulging muscles.

To her intense annoyance, it worked. She was riveted. How could anyone be so strong and yet unthreatening?

"Tell me, what would your friend say if she knew you had taken pleasure in watching her husband at his most vulnerable?"

"I didn't!" Branwen was outraged that he should even entertain the notion.

"Ah. So it was only me you ogled then." A corner of his lips curled up. "I'm flattered. Only, my masculine pride forces me to add that the temperature of the lake did not allow me to display myself at advantage. The cold tends to cause a man's, *intimate parts*, shall we say, to shrink somewhat. I usually look more impressive, or so I like to think."

There was nothing she could answer to that, because what she had seen had been impressive enough, and he knew it.

He started to walk to her slowly, a predator advancing on his prey. "So, will you answer my question, little raven, truthfully this time?"

"What question?" she croaked. He'd not *asked* her if she'd been ogling him, he'd assumed she had. And he'd been right. The image had haunted her every thought since.

"The skeletons in the ditch? Who do you think they were? There were no Englishmen in the area a hundred years ago, so we can rule out that possibility."

Those damned skeletons again! Irritation coursed down Branwen's veins. Why was he more interested in a pile of old bones than in the breathing, living woman in front of him? It was almost humiliating. Not that she wanted him to be interested in her, she reminded herself belatedly.

"You're obsessed!"

He made a face. "I'm intrigued—it's not quite the same. Some things in your country hold a fascination I cannot deny."

As he spoke, Matthew bridged the gap between them. She was now trapped, with her back against the wall, in the exact same place she'd been when she'd kissed her. She could not believe it was a coincidence. The man knew very well what he was doing. He meant to unsettle her and it was working.

He bit his bottom lip, and she suddenly understood the real

reason she had kissed him the other day. Because she had wanted to taste that perfect, luscious lip. It was as simple as that. She hadn't been able to make sense of the urge, because she had never felt it, but there was the explanation at last, the man held an undeniable fascination over her.

A dangerous fascination.

He leaned in toward her, eyes aglow. "Who are you, Branwen? What do you want with me?"

"Nothing. I just want ..."

I just want you.

The realization tore through her. Matthew was here, inches away from her. He was teasing her, but he was careful not to touch her. They were alone, they had already kissed once, and yet he was making no move to take advantage of her. Could she make that move? This was her best, perhaps her only chance to see what it felt like to be taken by a man who had not pounced on her, but had waited to be sure she was willing before allowing his desire to take over; it was her chance to take the initiative for once. There was a tingling in her body that was all new, a heaviness between her thighs proving her need to be filled. It was as far as she had ever come to experiencing desire for a man.

Should she act on it?

Could she?

Yes, perhaps. After reliving the assault she had been a victim of the day before, she thought she owed it to herself to at least try to see where this new desire would take her—here, now, with this man who posed no threat to her, this man who drew her irresistibly.

For years Branwen had told herself that if she one day met a man she desired, she would go with her instinct, that if she met a man who made her want to be taken, for once, she would not resist the impulse. It had seemed a harmless thought, one created to make her bear the touch of men she didn't want more easily, a way of assuring herself that she could one day regain control over her body, and allow someone she had actually chosen to enjoy what others had taken by force.

She had nothing to lose, no reputation to maintain, no husband's sensibility to preserve, barely any dignity left. She was already ruined ten times over. Why should she not allow herself what little satisfaction she could, try to prove to herself that she was just like the other women, that she too could feel desire for a man and act on it?

Such a thing had always seemed unattainable. But now ... Now it was not just an idle fantasy destined to make herself feel better. Now in front of her, there was a man staring at her as if he would devour her on the spot and yet did not push her, a real man of flesh and blood. Yes. Flesh, blood, and delicious skin, bulging muscles, silky hair, and tempting mouth.

Now she could make it happen and see.

The words passed her lips before she could think.

"I just want you."

The declaration sent a bolt of need shooting up Matthew's spine. Such a simple admission. Branwen wanted him, and he could tell that was no lie. Whoever had sent her and why did not matter. In that moment they were not enemies, they were just a man and a woman who wanted one another.

Desire flooded him and for the first time, he considered surrendering to it.

Usually when a woman stirred his desire, his first reaction was to recoil. His second was to wonder if it was worth the risk. His third was to steel himself so as not to be overcome.

Could he, just this once, with this woman who inflamed his blood like no other, act on his desire without overthinking it? Would he be able to stay in control if he allowed himself to do what he had never done before? He could not be sure.

"I want you too, but—"

"Sit."

One word. That was all it took to break through his resistance. That one word, the order to sit on the chair behind him. Never would he have taken the first step, in fact he'd been trying to convince himself that he was able to resist her lure, but just like she had with their kiss, Branwen wasn't leaving him any choice. There was a push against his chest and he fell, rather than sat on the chair waiting for him. A heartbeat later, Branwen was on his lap, bunching her skirts up in her hands.

His heart went to his throat. Was she really going to do this, here in the middle of the room, without even kissing him first? Then he felt her tug at the laces of his braies and his question was answered. Yes, apparently, she was. His shaft, hot and hard, was free before he even had time to tell her that he wanted to take it slower.

"Wait," he started. "We need to—"

"No. We need to do it now."

Before I lose my nerve. Before you come to your senses. Before someone comes in.

He wasn't sure which one she'd meant to say, but once again he was unable to contradict her. She was right. They needed to do it now, before they were interrupted or he expired from unfulfilled desire. Her fingers around him were too enticing, and he could feel her wetness at the tip of his cock. Despite the lack of seduction, she was ready, as ready as he was.

Branwen mumbled something in Welsh. It sounded like a plea. He could not believe it. Was she really begging him to let her do this?

There was no time to ask.

Without warning, she impaled herself on his shaft. Silky heat seared him, stealing his breath and causing his brain to explode. Matthew clenched his teeth. It was definitely too late to protest now, even if at the back of his mind he thought he might want to. Embedded as he was in scorching, feminine wetness, he could not think, he could only feel. And what he felt was so glorious he knew he would do nothing to stop her. He would sit, just as he'd been ordered, and allow himself to be taken.

Whatever she wished, he would grant her.

When Branwen grabbed his shoulders to steady herself while she rode him like a fierce Amazon warrior, he closed his fingers on her hips, intent on helping her along. Then he changed his mind and reached out to her bodice instead. He needed more, he needed to see and taste her, get his fill of her while she used him so deliciously. Her breasts, small and perfectly formed, were soon freed from the laces. White, with a rose-colored crown adorning them, they were just like he had pictured them during those solitary nights he'd spent pleasuring himself. With a groan he placed his lips on a puckered nipple, drawing it deep into his mouth. Jesus, he almost spilled there and then. So soft, so perfect. He could not get enough of her.

Wait! he wanted to cry out. *I'm not going to make it much further. I need to make the most of this.*

But he could not speak. His mouth was full of delicious woman and his brain had turned to mush.

As he released her nipple so he could give the other one the same attention, she let out a shuddering breath and her sheath fluttered around him. She was close. Thank God, because he knew he was about to erupt like never before. He just needed a little bit more time and he would make her—

She arched her back then, and squeezed her internal muscles a few times—and he was lost. A desperate cry reached his ears. His own or hers, he didn't know.

"Fuck, Branwen!"

The words leaving his mouth triggered his release. His skull exploded at the same time as his seed shot out of him in long, agonizing spurts. Nothing he'd experienced in his life could compare to the strength of that release. It sent ripples of ecstasy all the way to his toes and the roots of his hair.

For a long moment he stayed there, buried deep inside her, gasping for air, trying to make sense of what had just happened. He had not withdrawn, instead filling her with all he had. And though he knew he should be devastated, right now he cared not, for he could not even think.

All he wanted was to slide to the floor in a limp, sated mess. But he could not. Not yet.

"Wait, I need to ..." he rasped. "You didn't ... I need to see to your pleasure."

She made a face he had difficulty interpreting. Was she doubting his ability to satisfy her? The mere idea sent his blood boiling. He would make her lose her mind if it killed him, three, four times, if that was what it took to soothe his wounded pride.

"You don't need to do that," she said hurriedly, lifting herself off of him. He winced at the loss of her heat as well as the perfunctory way she acted. She was calm and collected, almost distant. He was still panting from the bewildering pleasure she'd milked from him and she was restoring order to her skirts and bodice as if nothing of importance had happened, as if he'd not been suckling her moments before, and had not emptied all he had inside her in a powerful rush. "It's all right."

All right? It was most decidedly not all right. Matthew didn't care to be considered like a selfish, incompetent lover, least of all by her.

"I will not be the only man who didn't make you come," he said through gritted teeth. He would be damned if she remembered this first time as anything less than earth-shattering. It had been, for him, but he needed it to be life-changing for her as well to be satisfied.

"You won't be the only one," she said, with what might have passed as a snort.

"Are Welshmen that bad?" he scoffed in turn. "Well, I won't have you think me the same as those self-centred, inept fools."

"Really, it's not a—" She stiffened when he stood up to draw her up to him. His body was still humming in desire, it would not take him long to be ready to take her again, this time on his terms. Perhaps he could make use of the table behind them, lay her down on it and spread her legs wide to plunge inside her silky depths. After all, he'd come inside her once already, so he might as well do it a second time. The damage had already been done. "Please, I need to go."

"You're not going anywhere until we are finished," he growled, tightening his hold around her waist.

"We are."

"I am, but *you*'re not."

"But you can't ..." She glanced down at his cock and gasped when she saw that it was still semi-hard. And little wonder. He had the most beautiful, most brazen woman he had ever seen in his arms, and she had just given him pleasure beyond his wildest imaginings.

"As you can see, we are far from done," he purred. "I can be hard again in moments, and anyway, I have my hands and mouth. Let me sit you on this table and show you that you don't have to go without. Then when I'm satisfied you have come enough times, we can pick things up where we left them."

A flurry of panic crossed her eyes, when he had expected them to catch ablaze. He had yet to meet a woman who did not like to be pleasured in that way. But Branwen reacted as if he had suggested he beat her up. What was going on? She might be working for someone else, but this reaction was not normal.

Branwen fought the panic rising in her chest. Matthew was not satisfied with having reached his release. Now he wanted to see to her pleasure, to "make her come," in his shocking words, and more than once. That had never happened before. Usually men were more than happy to accept her word that she didn't need more, and anyway, the majority of them didn't even notice she had not reached her pleasure, or care.

But Matthew, regardless of the strength of his release, seemed determined that she got her pleasure in turn. Whether it was a question of bruised masculine pride or genuine concern for her satisfaction, she wasn't sure, but either way she could not allow him to do it. She did not want to feel pleasure, she didn't want to prove *him* right.

Nausea flooded her throat, as it did every time she thought of *him*.

Oh, what had she done? She should have known this was a very bad idea, she should have guessed that it would not be as simple as taking the initiative and seeing where things went from there. She should not have been so presumptuous as to think she too could make love to a man she desired.

Taking her sudden immobility for a sign of surrender, Matthew placed his mouth in the crook of her neck. Everything within her leapt at the tender caress. Had he pounced on her, she would have pushed him away. Had he trapped her, she would have balked. But he had not pounced, he was wooing her, he had not trapped her, he was kissing her, coaxing her into surrender. And it was working.

Just as she was wondering how she was going to get out of this, the door of the solar burst open.

"Uncle Matthew!"

With a muttered curse Matthew turned around to hide his manhood, which, as he'd promised, had gone hard again.

"Jane." Too relieved at the girl's intervention to be embarrassed, Branwen drew her attention while he was putting order to his attire. Thankfully she was no longer sitting on him with her skirts up to her waist and his shaft deep inside her. "What are you doing on your own? Where's Siân?" The two sisters were rarely one without the other.

"I'm on my own because I want to surprise her. Uncle Matthew knows about my plan and he promised to help me."

"Well." She fully expected him to send his niece on her way with a curse so that the two of them could resume their lovemaking, but he surprised her by giving a reluctant chuckle, as if he could not believe the little girl had chosen this moment to come to him. A most unexpected reaction in a virile, aroused man.

"Yes, I did promise, didn't I?" He came to face Jane, a rueful smile on his lips. "Come on then, poppet, let's go."

Branwen had never seen a man so at ease with children. It would have been noteworthy enough if he'd been the little girl's father, but he was only her uncle. Not only that, but Jane was not a boy, the all-important heir to the family name. By rights, he shouldn't have cared about her.

But care he did. She watched as Jane threw herself in his arms and marveled at the transformation in the man. He'd gone from fiery lover to doting uncle in the blink of an eye. The tension in her body eased.

He would not touch her now. She would be able to leave the castle unchallenged, and try to make sense of what had just happened.

For a moment she thought she had gotten away with it, but before leaving, Matthew leaned in to murmur in her ear. "This isn't over, Raven. Next time I will make you come so hard you will not recognize yourself. I will make you scream so loud you won't be able to speak for days."

Yes, he would, if she let him.

And that was precisely the problem.

"Do you know who we haven't seen in a while? The Welsh girl. I wouldn't mind having another go at her. I'm fed up of having to use my own hand to ease the need in my cock."

"Oh, aye, me too. They're so callused half the time I rip at the flesh. Much better to make use of a woman's softness, is it not?"

The laughter following the crude declarations raised the hairs at the back of Matthew's neck. The guards stationed at Esgyrn Castle were not the most refined of men. They had been chosen for their loyalty to Connor and ability to fight, and these qualities did not always go hand in hand with a respectful attitude toward women, especially local ones, who were seen as little more than savages ready for the picking.

"What Welsh girl?" he asked, doing his best to appear calm. He hated to hear men speak thus, for it always put him in mind of his father, who would no doubt have balked at the idea of seeing to his needs with his own callused hands when there were plenty of low-born women around with whom he could satisfy his urges, and not worry about the consequences.

The men startled at his sudden appearance but quickly recovered.

"One of Lady Sheridan's friends. Not one of the noble ones, mind, for we can't even approach those. No, the one from the village, with dark hair and golden eyes," Thomas explained.

Welsh with golden eyes and dark hair. Living in the village. Not of noble birth. He knew of only one woman fitting that description. The men were talking about Branwen. Not only that, but they were talking about using her for their pleasure. Again.

Cold invaded him.

"You must have seen her around?" Owen added hopefully when he remained silent.

Oh, he had. He had done more than see her. Only the day before he'd been buried to the hilt inside her. "I have," he said through gritted teeth. "And so?"

"The woman is insatiable, she never says no. We had her together once, a few months ago," the man said, winking at his friend, who winked back. "I rode her hard and then Owen took my place. It aroused me so much to see him pumping away that I was hard again by the time he finished, so I had another turn. And did she utter a single word of protest? She did not. By the time we were through she was drenched with—"

"Yes, thank you," Matthew snapped, feeling sick. "I get it."

Far from being chastened, Thomas carried on. "When we told Eric about it, he made sure to go to her next time she visited the castle. And guess what she did? She sucked him dry at the back of the stables, no questions asked. The lucky bastard. Perhaps we should ask her ladyship to invite her—"

"Go back to your station! My brother doesn't pay you to bore me with your dubious exploits in bed." The two men glanced at each other uncomfortably, realizing they had gotten carried away, talking to their master's brother as if he were one of them. "And I suggest next time you see me, you remember who I am."

Matthew had heard enough. Branwen's behavior was properly scandalous, and everyone at the castle knew it. Everyone except him. The two men in front of him, and then that oaf Eric ... Who else knew about her fiery disposition? Who else had made the most of her willingness to offer men relief? Had she bedded the whole county? To think he'd wondered at her motivations for coming to him, and thought her at the pay of enemies! The truth was far simpler than he had feared. She was no spy working to gather information, no treacherous Welshman's ally, sent to lure him into danger. She was a promiscuous woman who slept with all the men who took her fancy, nothing more, nothing less. And in his inexperience, he had not seen it, instead imagining dark plots and dangerous schemes.

He remembered her telling him she was no virgin.

Well, no, apparently she was the very opposite of an innocent.

She'd avoided him after their kiss, she'd disappeared after riding him like an Amazon, before he could put a satisfactory end to the encounter. No more. He could not let her get away with making a fool out of him again and again, not when he had experienced something with her he had never experienced with any other woman, something he had sworn never to do before marriage. He had come inside her, for God's sake.

Well, yes, of course he had, she had not given him much choice. How was he supposed to resist when the seasoned temptress had squeezed him the way she had?

He was not going to allow a Welsh woman of all people to mess with his head and transform him into a pathetic figure of a man. True, his brother was happily married to a Welsh woman and deliriously happy. Matthew had to admit Esyllt was just as trustworthy and delightful as any Englishwoman, perhaps even more so, but still.

A man had his pride, and Branwen would not avoid him a third time. After their passionate encounter in the solar, she had slipped away from the castle while he'd been busy with Jane, even though he'd made clear his intention to see to her needs. When he'd joined Esyllt and Connor late in the afternoon, they'd told him Branwen had gone back to the village. His little bird, an unlikely white raven, had flown away.

Well, he would make sure to catch her again.

Chapter Four

A bird landed on the branch next to him. At first Matthew thought it was a dove or a white pigeon, nothing out of the ordinary. Then he looked more closely when the animal let out a frightful croak. A croak no dove or pigeon would ever make.

"I'll be damned," he said between his teeth.

"I'm sorry, what was that?" Esyllt asked, turning toward him.

"Nothing. Forgive me." He should not have used those crude words in a lady's presence. If Connor had been here, he would have remonstrated with him for using that kind of language in front of his wife. "Only I saw a white raven in that tree. It took me by surprise. I had never seen one of them before, hadn't even believed such birds could exist."

"No, me neither." She looked in the direction he was indicating and watched as the bird flew away with a series of indignant squawks, as if annoyed humans dared to talk about him. "How odd that we should see one so close to Branwen's cottage when they are so rare. Her name means 'white raven', you know." Matthew clenched his fists. Yes, he did know. "Or 'beautiful raven', it depends."

Beautiful. That he could agree with. So beautiful she drew men like a moth to a flame, before consuming them with her inner heat one after the other. The question he'd asked himself time and time again since the day before flashed through his mind once more. How many men had she welcomed inside her body?

How big of a fool was he to have been taken in by her brazen ways?

Grunting, he nudged his horse further away from his sister-in-law's mare. Perhaps they had better not talk, for what would she reveal about her friend next? That she was the kindest of souls? That she'd lost three husbands in suspicious circumstances? He didn't want to hear anything positive about Branwen when his mood was so dark, and he feared hearing more vile revelations when he was already seething. It was therefore best to stay silent.

What he would have liked was to urge his mount into a reckless gallop, to try and ease away the tension in his body, but anything other than a walk was out of the question. Esyllt was due to give birth any day now, he could not cause her any discomfort just because he was angry. It was already quite a feat for her to be on horseback at this late stage, but she had insisted on accompanying him to the village when he'd told her that was where he was going. He had tried to backtrack and say that he might not spend a lot of time in the actual village, but she had insisted she wanted to see her friend, to check how she was after her fainting spell. There had been no way to dissuade her, and he could not let her ride unescorted.

They soon reached the village nestled at the foot of the hill.

As he was helping Esyllt down from the saddle, a woman

came to speak to her in rapid Welsh. She was obviously congratulating her lady on the impending birth, but Matthew was not able to understand much of the conversation. He did his best not to betray any impatience, but it must have shown on his face, for after a while, Esyllt took pity on him.

"Go ahead. I will join you in a moment."

Matthew did not need to be told twice. This was even better. The conversation he wanted to have with Branwen didn't need any witnesses. He headed toward her cottage—and almost collided with a man walking out of the door. When he nodded, Matthew recognized him as one of the Englishmen stationed in town. His breathing was labored and his long hair somewhat ruffled.

"Come to take your turn, have you?" He let out a laugh and winked. "You might want to wait a moment, give the poor girl a respite."

"The girl?" Matthew repeated stupidly.

"In the hut. God knows what her name is. Probably something neither of us can get our tongue around. Fortunately, uttering foreign sounds is not the only thing she can do with that mouth of hers."

Matthew recoiled. That man had just been fucking Branwen? And he thought he was next? He had never felt dirtier—or more foolish.

Without addressing a single word to the vile man for fear he would throttle him on the spot, he stormed inside the cottage. He could not ignore it anymore; he'd been completely wrong about her motives for coming to him. Branwen didn't pose any danger to his life, only to his pride. She didn't work for someone who wanted him dead, she only seduced all the men she could find with shocking disregard for modesty.

He found her by the window, pale and trembling, when he

had imagined she would be as ruddy-faced and out of breath as her English lover. When she saw him, she paled further. Ah, so she hadn't counted on him finding out just how debauched she was and didn't like to have to admit to it out loud.

Too bad.

"I just met your friend," he said, throwing her a look he hoped conveyed his disgust.

"M-my friend?"

"Forgive me, perhaps I should say your *lover*. Did you give the poor man a chance to make you come?" he snarled, remembering how she had denied him the right to make her reach her peak. She must have found him lacking, and unworthy of the honor, for what would be the point of bedding all the men she could find if not to feel pleasure? "He was very complimentary of your skills at any rate. Perhaps I should see for myself what it is you can do with that pretty mouth of yours. Since you don't care about the pleasure I want to give you, why should I worry about it? I should just use you for my own relief."

Branwen placed a hand against the wall, as if to steady herself. "It's not what you think."

"Are you saying that the man coming out of your cottage panting and sweating didn't just fuck you?" He glanced toward the pallet in the corner. It was neatly made and there wasn't a crease on the blanket. So they had not used it for their tryst. Then what? The chair, like she had with him in the solar? The table? "Did he take you up against the wall like a whore? Is that how you like it?" He took a step toward her.

"No, it's not. Please, stop talking to me thus."

"How should I talk to you?" He took another step toward her. They were now within touching distance of each other and he made a conscious effort not to reach out to her. "Do you want me to woo you beforehand, is that what it is? Why? There was no need last time. You just lifted your skirts and sheathed my cock inside your cunt before I had time to utter a sound." The crude words passed his lips without providing him any relief from the disillusion churning in his guts. "What would you like today? Shall I take you where you stand?"

"Matthew, please. You ... You're frightening me."

The words were like a slap. He'd never frightened a woman in his life before. Men, aye, many, for a variety of reasons. But women ... He had never caused any to look at him with eyes wide with fear. He took a closer look at Branwen.

Christ on the cross, was she crying?

He took a step back, horrified at his behavior. Who was this man, talking to a woman about using her mouth for his selfish pleasure, calling her a whore? Using foul language to describe what they had done? Backing her up into a corner, while threatening to fuck her against the wall in anger?

No wonder she was as pale as a corpse, and scared of what he might do. He was furious, but that was no excuse.

"I—"

Just then the door opened behind him. Damnation, this had to be Esyllt, finally free of the villager congratulating her. Cursing his luck, Matthew turned to face her, intent on asking her to give them a moment's privacy. The conversation needed to take a different turn. He needed to calm down, show Branwen he was not dangerous. He needed answers, and this was not the way to get them.

"My lady," he said, doing his best to sound calm. "Would you mind—" Her grimace stopped him mid-sentence. "What is it?"

"I think ..." She stopped and stared at him in horror, then at the place between her feet. Matthew followed her gaze and saw that the earthen floor under her skirts was wet. "I think my waters just broke."

Branwen rushed over to her friend, both worried for her and relieved at the interruption. Matthew had been out of his mind with fury, hatred, or lust, she wasn't sure quite which. What was certain was that there had been a mad glint in his eyes and he'd used language the likes of which she had never heard before. It would have been hard to face him in normal circumstances, but after the Englishman's assault, it was unbearable. Her life, never an easy one, had just taken a turn for the worst.

"Are you in pain?" she asked Esyllt, forcing herself to focus on the other woman's predicament. Now was not the time to dwell on her pitiful situation.

"No, but I think the baby might be coming." Her friend gave her a watery smile. "We all know what that means when a woman's waters break, don't we?"

Yes, they did. Esyllt could not ride back to Castell Esgyrn or go anywhere in that state. She would have to stay here until they knew what was happening.

Taking her by the elbow, Branwen led her to her pallet.

"Lie down. I will go get Ffion. She will be able to examine you, and tell us how things are progressing."

"Go get Connor first," Esyllt panted. "I need him."

"Connor will be no use to you right now, we had better—"

"I will get him."

To Branwen's relief, Matthew stepped forward, intent on helping. But, of course, he knew that his brother would want to be with his wife at this difficult time. After losing his first wife and babe in childbed, he would never allow Esyllt to face the birth alone. It was already a miracle he had allowed her so far from the castle when she was so near her term.

"I will go to this Ffion on my way, if Branwen tells me where to find her, and then I will ride straight to Esgyrn Castle. On Midnight's back it won't take me long. I'll bring Connor back to you before you know it."

"Don't ..." Esyllt clutched at her stomach. "Don't let him worry unduly. He will be—"

"I know, but it will be all right," Matthew soothed. He surprised Branwen, Esyllt, and perhaps even himself by placing a hand on his sister-in-law's head in a paternal gesture. "Now, lie down and let me go get the woman you need."

Branwen stared. Was this really the same man she'd faced in all his ire only moments ago?

Just like she had the other day when Jane had walked in on them moments after he'd achieved his release, she marveled at his ability to dissemble. Before Esyllt's arrival, he'd been like a demon possessed, speaking to her in the crudest of terms. For a moment she had wondered if he would not assault her, up against the wall, as he'd threatened to do, and now he was the calm and reassuring presence Esyllt needed to keep panic at bay. This was even more remarkable that he'd been less than accepting of his sister-in-law at first. But now there was no more ardent supporter of her.

What would it feel like to have such a man at her side, Branwen wondered? If he was as fierce in love and protection as he was in accusation and suspicion, then she would have nothing to worry about for the rest of her life.

Unfortunately, he was as likely to want her in it as he was to want someone to poke a hole in his chest.

"I'll be back in no time," he told Esyllt, before turning back to face her. His eyes were two glittering gems. "Now tell me where to find this Ffion."

~

"What the hell were you *thinking*?" Connor roared. "Bringing my wife, my pregnant wife, into your debauched life?"

"Debauched?" Matthew repeated, incredulous. The word could hardly apply to his life and they both knew it.

But his brother was beside himself with worry, and past all reasoning. "Don't play the innocent with me. Why would you go to see someone you kissed so passionately if not to bed her? Well, next time you feel the urge to fuck a woman, kindly leave my wife out of it, even if that woman is her friend, do you hear!"

Matthew gritted his teeth and stayed silent under the onslaught, knowing deep down Connor needed an outlet for his fear. This wasn't really about him taking Esyllt anywhere or fucking anyone, it wasn't about him at all.

His brother was merely petrified of hearing that the dreaded moment had come. After what had happened with Helen, such a reaction was all too understandable. He would be out of his mind with fear at the idea of losing another wife in childbirth, this time one he loved more than life itself.

Against all odds, Connor had fallen in love with the woman he had been forced to marry, and Matthew himself, despite his initial reluctance, had come to respect and love Esyllt. He didn't want to lose her either, but it was different. Because he didn't love her in that way, he was able to hold on to his sanity and see that the birth did not have to end up in disaster. Not all women died in childbed, thankfully, and his sister-in-law had borne a child already, with no complications. There was no reason to think this birth would be any different. He just needed to reassure his brother.

"Esyllt asked me to tell you everything was progressing normally, that you weren't to worry overmuch," he said, knowing how this information would be received.

"Oh, did she really?"

"Yes. Now come. I've already asked for Storm to be saddled. I'll take you to her. She asked after you."

He didn't need to say more. Connor flew out of the door. A moment later they were both thundering through the castle gate, heading for Branwen's cottage.

Chapter Five

"Another daughter." Matthew smiled at the new mother holding her child in her arms. "Didn't I tell you? My brother can only father girls."

The said brother would have glared at him for this sally if Esyllt had not placed a soothing hand on his arm and smiled back. "Another girl is just perfect. She's perfect."

"She is. All that remains to be seen is if I was right about the color of her eyes." He had once predicted that the babe would have green eyes, just like her two parents. He was more convinced than ever that it would be the case, but they would have to wait a few months to be sure. "I think the same shade as yours, my lady, would be the most fetching. Connor's eyes could all too easily be mistaken for a snake's. Useful to instill fear into your opponents if you're a knight, but less becoming in a woman, don't you think?"

"Will you cease your blabbering and give my wife and me a moment's privacy so we can get acquainted with our new daughter?" Connor growled. The gruffness would take a moment to fade away. He had barely recovered from the shock of being told Esyllt had already been delivered of the child when they'd reached the cottage. Then the relief of seeing that both his girls were doing well had almost floored him.

"Of course. Take all the time you need."

After one last glance at his new niece, Matthew left the cottage.

Outside, he found Branwen in a most unexpected position. Sitting on the bench next to the vegetable patch, she was hugging herself. He had expected her to be delighted with her friend's happy deliverance but she looked about to cry. Again. The sight unsettled him. He would never have thought a bold vixen like her would exhibit such vulnerability, but she seemed oddly prone to crying and fainting, like a woman constantly on edge. What was making her so overwrought?

When she saw him, she stiffened, as if caught doing something forbidden. "You're here," she said in a flat tone.

He arched a brow. Of course he was. He'd been there only a moment ago. "Where else would I be?"

"England, where you really want to be?" she suggested with no small amount of bitterness.

Mm. He didn't quite know what to answer to that. Did he really want to be in England? A few months ago, he would have said yes. Now he was not so sure.

"You'll have to wait a moment to get your home back, I'm afraid," he informed her, not knowing what to say to this new Branwen. The fearless minx he could handle, but he was at a loss in front of the vulnerable woman. "Connor will want to assure himself all is well before he allows his wife to go anywhere, but I'm sure they would let you stay with her if you wished."

She stood up, her face hardening. All traces of vulnerability had disappeared, replaced by a cold indifference he guessed she used as a shield. "I'd rather not stay while they're here. Esyllt will understand. She knows I don't like to be around babies. But it matters not. I can always find another place to sleep tonight."

At that, Matthew remembered what had transpired earlier that day. In the drama that had followed, he'd quite forgotten it. But of course, Branwen had been exposed for the wanton she was by the Englishman leaving her cottage still panting from exertion.

He scoffed. She'd said she could find another place for the night, and he could well believe it. She could probably take her pick of men who would offer her shelter, men who would be amply compensated for their generosity when she used her talented mouth on them as a reward. The notion had his blood boiling.

"No, I do not doubt you can find a bed to lie in, even if I'm not sure there will be much sleeping in it. But do you know?" he jeered, "for someone who doesn't like children, you place yourself at serious risk of carrying your own one day, one whose father's identity you won't even know."

Her lips trembled, betraying the anger simmering under the detached surface, but Matthew knew the accusation was not untoward. Why, in nine months from now she could well give birth to his …

He stopped the thought before it could fully form. Even if she had fallen with child from their encounter in the solar, as he'd said, neither he nor she would know for sure he was the father, since less than two days later she'd bedded one of the Englishmen from town. And it was probably not all. Who knew how many men she had taken to her bed since she'd last bled? Any of them could be the father if she gave birth to a babe at the end of the year. And it was for the best he would never know whether their lovemaking had borne fruit, Matthew reminded himself. He didn't want a bastard child anyway.

"I see you are still intent on insulting me?" Branwen said through gritted teeth.

"I'm not insulting you. I'm stating facts." He was not impressed by her outrage. She might not know what Owen and Thomas had revealed about her, but she could not deny having been found moments after having bedded a man. "Don't tell me you've already forgotten that when I came to visit earlier, I walked into another man exiting your cottage after—"

"What we did is none of your concern."

"It is if he is going to assume I will fuck you while his seed is still inside you," Matthew snapped back. "Tell me, just so I know how big of a fool I am, *did* he make you come? Or did you send him on his way before he could, like you did with me?"

Matthew berated himself for insisting thus. Why did he need to know? It was infuriating, and only went to show that he was a fool, but he could not let it go. Why had she denied him the chance to give her the pleasure she was clearly after?

Arglwydd Mawr!

Branwen bristled. How could Matthew be so scathing? Where was the man who'd spoken so tenderly to Esyllt only moments ago and looked at her babe with awe in his eyes? The sight had torn at her heart, because it proved beyond question that he could be kind and loving.

Only he chose not to be with her, because he thought she didn't deserve it.

With her, he was his arrogant, unbearable self.

"I have no wish to discuss this with you." Not now, not after having seen her friend give birth, and then present the healthy babe to her beloved, awe-struck husband, not while her skin was still burning from the touch of another man, not when she was so confused about her feelings toward Matthew, not ever.

"But I might wish to discuss it with you," he said, straightening up to his full, impressive height. "That's why I came to see you today, to have an explanation. Yesterday I heard two men at the castle talking about you and how you serviced them both at the same time."

Something died within her. She knew very well to whom he was referring, even if she didn't know the men's names. Thankfully, so far, the two guards at Castell Esgyrn had been the only ones demanding to share her in that way. The idea of Matthew hearing about this, thinking that she made a habit of allowing two men to possess her together made her sick. Would there be no end to her humiliation?

"Well, what of it? You thought you were special, is that what it is?" she cried out, deciding the only way she could bear this was to make him feel as bad as she felt. "But you are not the only man I've had, far from it. I never lied to you, I told you I was no virgin, didn't I? Yet you didn't let it deter you. So don't come complaining now that I have a past."

From the way he recoiled, she could tell she had hit a nerve. It spurred her on. Let him get what he deserved for making her feel so wretched. Why should she try to spare him when he was being so cruel toward her?

"Admit it, this is not about me but about you and your pride," she carried on. "You don't like to hear that you didn't give me pleasure because it makes you feel like an inferior lover. You don't want to hear that I bed other men because it makes it obvious that you are just one of many when you thought you were unique. But tell me, why am I supposed to care about your feelings? You are nothing to me, just another Englishman thinking he can have it all."

That was her bitterness talking, because in truth she had never thought that of him.

"When have I ever given you the impression I was like that?" he growled, taking her by the elbow. She should have tried to free herself, but oddly, the gesture did not scare her.

Enough men had acted aggressively toward her over the years for her to know the difference. Matthew was not about to hurt her, he simply wanted to understand what had happened. "*I* was not the one who initiated our first kiss. *I* did not push you down into the chair to ride you that day in the solar. It seems to me that if one of us takes what they want, it is *you*."

He was right. She had acted selfishly, taking what she wanted regardless of his opinion. Not that he had put up much of a fight. Still, she felt in the wrong, because she been the one initiating it—both times.

Shame made her lash out.

"Why are you here? Have you come to insult me or fuck me? I'd like to know, so I can prepare myself."

The crude word exploded between them. For a moment she feared he would tumble her onto the ground, and plunge deep inside her, just to make her regret the taunt. Had she been too presumptuous in thinking he posed no threat to her? He was a man, and earlier today he had talked about using her in the crudest way.

"I came here to have answers," Matthew said, releasing Branwen's elbow as fast as if it had burned him.

Have you come here to fuck me?

Hearing the shocking word in her mouth had made him want to do just that. How could that be? He was mad at her, he should not be thinking of her in that way, not when she had explained he was just one of many, not special in any way, and unable to give her pleasure. He should be humiliated by her tirade, not aroused!

This was all infuriating.

"You want answers? You want explanations?" Branwen snarled. "About what? My inability to come? About the numbers of men I've been forced to service? You want to know why I cannot feel pleasure in a man's arms, is that what it is?"

She sounded like she had never sounded before, and once again, she looked about to cry.

Matthew stilled as white-hot anger was replaced by icy dread. This conversation was taking a turn he had not expected.

"What do you mean?" he asked with deadly calm. Had she just said "men she had been *forced* to service?" That was what he wanted to know, but when she answered, she focused on the last part of her confession.

"I can't feel pleasure in a man's arms because I will not let it happen, that's why! I cannot. If I do, he will be proven right."

"Who will be proven right?" The more she talked, the less he understood what she was saying, and the more worried he became.

"He thinks ... he said ... 'Listen to you moaning. You like what I'm doing to you, don't you?' But I didn't! I didn't, do you hear? I swear it, I didn't like it! I never do."

Dear God, whom was she taking about? The Englishman from earlier? Had he praised her responsiveness as a lover while he was taking her? But why would it be a problem for her to moan under his caresses? Surely that was normal, even desirable? Flattering? Something was very wrong and he needed to get to the bottom of it.

"Branwen, answer me. What on earth are you talking about?"

He grabbed her by the shoulders, barely resisting the urge to shake her. She seemed not to notice he was here, exactly like that time by the barbican when George and Elena had been fighting. There was a dazed expression on her face, as if she didn't know where she was. She wavered on her feet, her body losing all of its tension. In a moment she might ...

Matthew braced himself, knowing what was coming. A heartbeat later, Branwen fell into his arms, unconscious.

"Thank God. Finally, you're awake." Esyllt's voice, quivering with relief.

"Where am I?" Her own, slightly slurred.

"In your cottage."

Branwen blinked and looked around, trying to make sense of what had happened. The last thing she remembered was being outside by the vegetable patch with Matthew. She was now inside the cottage, lying on a blanket next to the pallet where Esyllt sat with her daughter in her arms. No doubt Matthew had been the one carrying her there, just like he had the day she had jumped on George. It seemed that for the second time in as many weeks she had fainted in his arms. What would he be thinking?

Did it matter? He already thought her the most shameless whore. After that, it would make little difference if he thought her a pathetic, weak female.

"You're all right, Branwen, I'm here. You're safe," Esyllt told her before lifting her head to the men standing over them, concern etched on their faces. "Would you two please give us a moment?"

Connor glanced at his wife, then at his brother, who was scowling. He nodded and dragged him outside by the elbow. It was obvious Matthew didn't want to go and was hoping she would ask him to stay, but Branwen kept her gaze on her friend, because she did want him to go. She did not want to see him now.

And preferably never again.

He would only insult her, and cause her to feel worse than anyone had made her feel, maybe faint again. She could not allow it. Whatever he thought, she did not deserve to be treated thus.

"What happened this time?" Esyllt asked when the door had closed. "Did you see the man who attacked you as a child, while you were out there with Matthew? Is that why you fainted?"

Branwen shook her head. She could not tell her friend what had transpired between her and her brother-in-law. Esyllt knew about the kiss, but not what had happened in the solar, or the awful arguments. It was better that way. After months of enmity the two of them had finally reached an agreement, Branwen could not now give her friend reason to think ill of her husband's brother.

"No. I haven't seen the man for years, since …"

Not since the assault in the clearing, she meant. At first she had feared he might try to find out where she lived, come to her again, but he had not once approached the village. She would have been relieved had she not concluded it was because he had found other young girls to assault. She had not been special to him, he'd not had any feelings toward her, he'd only wanted to slake his passing lust. He didn't need her for that, with so many other virgins around. The idea that he must have ruined dozens of lives was sickening.

Esyllt didn't comment, but she was still waiting for an explanation.

"I haven't had anything to eat all day, that may be why I fainted," Branwen said, hoping this would be enough to placate her.

It wasn't, not if the look in her eyes was any indication, but mercifully, she pretended to believe the explanation.

"I will ask Connor to get some food for us. I could do with eating something myself. While we eat, we will discuss what arrangements can be made for the night. I'm sorry to say that Connor has already told me he would not allow me to go anywhere for the next two days at the very least. And naturally, he will stay by my side." Esyllt gave a sigh. "So I'm afraid your cottage will—"

"It's not an issue. Don't worry, I had already anticipated I would need to leave for a few days," Branwen soothed.

Or rather, Matthew had already warned her she would have to find another bed to lie in, and assumed she would entertain a lover in it.

She would have liked to stay, if only to make him regret his untoward accusations but she could not. It would be torture to have to witness the new parents' delight, to see in their eyes the love they had for their newly born babe and each other.

Branwen gave the sleeping little girl a stroke on the cheek as the familiar pangs of regret tore through her gut. What she wouldn't give to hold her own child one day. But it was an impossible dream. Women like her didn't deserve to bear children who would only be mocked and reviled. It would not be fair on them. So she simply had to forget her own desire and needs.

"But this is your home," Esyllt protested. "Where will you go?"

"To my mother's. Don't worry about it. You and little Gwenllian take all the time you need. I'll be fine."

Yes. At least that was the hope.

Chapter Six

Why could he not stay away from the infuriating woman, Matthew wondered, even as he steered Midnight onto the south road. Esyllt and her daughter had barely been back at Esgyrn Castle a day, and here he was already, riding toward the village—and Branwen.

They had not seen one another since the day she had fainted in his arms outside her cottage, and he didn't like the way they had left things. Her words had raised too many questions. Who the hell had she been talking about when she'd said he could not prove him right? And try as he may, he just couldn't forget she'd said she'd been *forced* to service men.

This was not the kind of declaration one could ignore.

As he saw the first house nestled in the riverbend, he started to wonder. Would he find another man in the cottage today? What would he do if he did? Would he be able to stop himself from strangling him on the spot, especially if the bastard asked him if he had come to take his turn? He couldn't be sure.

Worse, would he catch the two lovers in the act? Would he hear Branwen's cries of pleasure as he approached? Everything within him rebelled at the thought. It might be better to turn around while he still could.

He pushed on, and a moment later, he had reached the cottage.

There was no man in front of the door, he was relieved to see, but a woman. She was not the one he had thought to find, even if, admittedly, she did bear a resemblance to her. He did not need her to introduce herself to understand that she was a relative of Branwen's, perhaps even her sister.

"Good morning," he said, less cordially than he should have. But really, never had a man's patience been more sorely tested. Whenever he wanted a conversation with Branwen, he seemed to be thwarted. Where was she? This was her home. If anyone should be there, it was she.

The girl looked at him as if he'd just spoken in a foreign tongue. Which, of course, he had. Evidently, she did not share her sister's knowledge of English. Although ... he'd hardly said anything elaborate. Anyone in their right mind would have guessed he was greeting her. This was getting worse and worse.

"*Bore da*," he repeated, calling on what little Welsh he'd picked up since his arrival. "*Lle mae* Branwen?"

Despite his efforts, the girl did not appear to understand him any better. He sent a stone flying with a kick, not even trying to repress his frustration. What had he done to deserve this? He only wanted to know where Branwen was. It shouldn't be that difficult. Would he forever be denied where the Welsh woman was concerned?

"What's the matter with you, can't you understand a simple sentence?" he muttered, refusing to consider that he might be the one at fault. The woman should have understood him. Even if he'd somehow mispronounced the words, surely, his meaning would be clear? This was Branwen's home, was it not? What else could he be asking?

"Don't you dare mock her, do you hear, English! You can insult *me* all you want, but don't you dare mock my sister."

The woman he'd been looking for was suddenly standing behind him, a basket full of wizened apples in her hands and a look of fury such as he had never seen etched on her face. Even when he had walked in on her fresh from a man's arms and called her a whore, she had not been so irate. In her anger, she seemed a foot taller. Magnificent, like a goddess of wrath. Matthew blinked, determined not to let her beauty impress him.

"Mock her?" He'd not been mocking the girl precisely, only expressing his frustration at being denied a simple thing, to see Branwen. "I didn't mock her."

"Don't you try to be clever with me. I heard you ask what was wrong with her."

Well, yes, he had, but that was not the same. "I didn't mean—"

"Enough!"

Branwen was beside herself with fury and disappointment. What was Matthew doing here? She had thought never to see him again, and had worked very hard at telling herself it was for the best. But not only had he come back mere days after having left, but he had started to mock Eirwen. Tears stung her eyes. He was just as predictable and nasty as the others. Why was she even surprised?

Before she could lash out, she turned to her sister, who was looking at them with confusion on her face. "Stay here a moment, please. Everything's fine but I need a word alone with the man. Sit on the bench and wait for me. I won't be long."

Eirwen nodded and took her place on the bench. Branwen handed her the best of the apples she'd gathered then pushed Matthew toward the cottage. Fortunately, for she was not in the mood to argue, he complied readily enough.

"What did you do to her?" she roared, turning to him as

soon as the door was closed. It was one thing insulting her, but to attack her innocent sister was unforgivable. She would never have thought him capable of such villainy.

"*Do* to her?" He sounded nonplussed, and not a little vexed by the question. "I didn't do anything. I asked her where you were. In Welsh no less. And she looked at me as if I made no sense."

His explanation, so simple and delivered in such a guileless manner, deflated her anger. It seemed she had been wrong, and he hadn't meant to mock her sister. Feeling utterly silly for having jumped to conclusions, she placed her basket on the table, to try and give herself time to compose herself.

"She was confused because she ... because ..." She stopped, unable to say it. Matthew might not have meant any harm, but he would for certain mock her if he knew. "Why are you here?" she asked instead.

There was a long pause. Then, he answered, his voice huskier than usual. "I don't know."

This extraordinary answer doused the last embers of her anger. He looked genuinely puzzled as to what had made him come, and not best pleased about it, as if he would have preferred to wash his hands of her. But life was not like that. It had a way of forcing you to confront ugly things. She should know, so she could not help but sympathize with him.

"I think you came here for answers," she murmured. "Just like the other day."

At least she hoped that was why he was here, because she would not be satisfied until he knew the real reason why she bedded all these men. She needed to tell him what the situation was, and save what little dignity and self-worth she had left. Though she was loath to discuss such an intimate thing, the alternative was to have him believing her the most despicable wanton, so it was better to have the truth out. Despite the harshness he'd demonstrated toward her the other day, she sensed that if he knew the reason behind the Englishman's presence in her cottage, Matthew would sympathize with her. Esyllt had told her he was nothing like the cold man he appeared to be at first glance and she believed it.

In any case, nothing she said now would not make this any worse, so she had nothing to lose.

Brown eyes pierced her all the way to her soul. "You're right. I do want answers."

Very well, but how could she start?

"I'm not who you think I am," she said, almost exactly the same thing she had told Esyllt. "I ... I do bed men, but it's not for my pleasure. It has never been for my pleasure."

Matthew couldn't have explained why that was, but he knew instantly that whatever Branwen told him from now on, however odd, however unpleasant, would be the absolute truth.

He asked the first question that came to his mind. "Why did you bed me then?" It was what he had obsessed about for days and he needed to know, uncomfortable as it was to discuss such matters.

She hesitated, too long for his liking. "Usually, I bed men against my will. With you it was more complicated." Well, that was not exactly the answer he'd wanted to hear, or flattering, but he couldn't complain, not when he'd asked for it. Feeling more unsettled than ever, he waited, hoping there was more to it. "I am trapped in a situation where everyone thinks I'm a wanton, when I would like nothing more than to still be a virgin and lead a life free of men."

There was a pause, then Matthew said. "This is all about your sister, is it not?"

Why he could make such an assertion, he wasn't sure, but suddenly it seemed clear to him. Branwen had glanced toward the door, and the place where the girl was waiting, when she'd said she wished she could live a life free of men. Somehow this had to be linked to her sister in her mind. But how?

She nodded, proving he'd guessed correctly.

"It all started because I had to protect her. She is different from the rest of us, as you noticed." Matthew wasn't sure he was expected to confirm it, but he had indeed seen that the girl's reactions were slower. "She's always been like that. The midwife who attended my mother when she was born said the birth had been long and complicated. My sister was stuck, and because of it, her mind has never been able to develop in the same way as other people's. For all that, she is the loveliest, most loving person I know."

"Of course. I'm sorry," Matthew said inadequately. What was he supposed to say to that? He had no idea. He'd never met anyone in that situation.

"She doesn't understand things as we do, often doesn't know how to react. But even if she did, she wouldn't have deserved to be treated thus."

There was a pause and Matthew braced himself. They were coming to the heart of the matter. What was she about to reveal? Whatever it was, he sensed it would haunt his thoughts for days. "Treated how, Branwen?" he asked in a whisper.

"One day, years ago, I came home to find her on her own with a stranger old enough to be our father. He was trying to ... he was ..." Another pause. He waited, even if he could guess all too well what the man had been trying to do. Bile rose in his throat. How could anyone be so depraved as to attack a girl who had no idea what was going on? "I couldn't let him do it. I was already ruined so I ... I offered myself instead. It was the only way. At least *I* understood what was happening."

Yes, unlike her sister, *she* would have understood all too well she was being raped. Everything within him surged in hatred and he wished he had the man before him so he could make him pay for his villainy. Then he registered her choice of words. She'd said she'd already been ruined, not that she had already bedded a man. This suggested the previous encounter had happened against her will as well.

"How come you weren't a virgin?" he asked, thinking at this point that they were past the awkwardness such a question created.

Branwen swallowed. "A few years before that, a man saw me one day in the forest and ..."

And raped her. Matthew rubbed a hand over his face, appalled. "Dear God, Branwen ... How old were you when the man attacked your sister?"

"Seventeen."

"Jesus." At seventeen she'd already been raped? And how old had her sister been then? Little more than a child, surely, for she was more than a couple of years younger than her, by the look of things. How much more appalling could all this get?

"Anyway, once the man saw that I was willing, he let her go and—"

"Willing!" Matthew spluttered. "How the devil did he get the idea that you were willing?"

"Because of what I ... because of what I did to him." She lowered her eyes and gave a shiver of revulsion.

"Listen to me," he said sternly, intent on making her understand she was a victim in the whole affair, not a willing participant. "A man knows when the woman in his arms is there reluctantly. That bastard had no excuse to go to your sister, who was a child and could not possibly want him, and then to pretend that you knelt at his feet because you wanted to. He might not have used physical force on you, but what he did is just as bad. He knew you only did what you did to spare an innocent from his advances, and he took advantage of it knowingly, instead of drowning in shame and self-loathing as he should have done."

Christ on the cross, he had rarely heard a more sordid tale.

Now he understood why Branwen had always seemed oddly innocent and ill at ease in front of him, despite her supposed depravity, why she'd not been able to explain the urge to kiss him. She was new to all this. All her interactions with men had been imposed on her.

"How many of those men has there been over the years?" he asked through gritted teeth.

Everything was starting to make sense. The way she had pounced on him earlier and immediately assumed he had been trying to hurt her sister, the look of despair and shame after the Englishman had left her cottage the other day, certainly not the way a sated woman looked. She had been pale and teary, like a woman who'd just been raped.

She had even told him as much.

How many men I've been forced to service.

And he'd ignored her words. He was sick to his soul, thoroughly disgusted with himself. Instead of letting his pride have the upper hand, he should have asked her if she was all right, and then run straight back outside to ram his fist down the man's throat.

He had barged in like the ignorant boor he was, accusing her of being little more than a whore, and asking if she preferred he used her mouth or take her up against the wall.

Oh, God, it didn't bear thinking about.

"How many?" he repeated, resisting the urge to take her hand in his.

She flushed crimson, as if hating that he had guessed what she had done to the man—and countless others. Well, he hated it too, the knowledge that she had been subjected to such treatment from men who'd been too selfish and dishonorable to ignore her distress because they wanted relief. Men like Thomas and Owen who had appeased their conscience with the fact that she had not protested.

"I-I don't know." Everything froze within Matthew. There had been so many that she did not even know. That was the worst answer she could have given him. "The next one came to find me as I was washing in the stream the following week, telling me he'd heard about me from his friend, the one after that claimed he'd seen us by the river bank and wanted the same. Since then it has never stopped."

No. It had not stopped. For years and years she'd been a victim of men who were too blinded by lust to accept or even consider she might be unwilling.

"You don't tell them you don't want them?" He did his best not to sound accusatory, because it was not his intention to make her feel bad. He only meant to understand the extent of her predicament.

She shook her head, as if she'd tried this more often than she could think, in vain.

"It's always worse in the end if you struggle. Then they make you pay for your defiance, possess you in the most animalistic way possible, just to show you what they can do. And it hurts even more." Matthew's blood was now frozen in his veins. "I learned the hard way it was better not to protest, so I just let them ... do what they want, however they want. With the town now teeming with Englishmen it's worse than it ever was. I know countless women who have been damaged beyond repair because they tried to fight their attackers. I don't want to be the next one. If I allow them to take their pleasure, then at least they don't treat me too badly. But if I can get away with not allowing them to enter my body, I will. Sometimes if I'm lucky, my hand is enough, but more often than not I—"

"Please, you don't have to tell me," Matthew interrupted, appalled.

More often than not, she used her mouth. The guards had said as much, when describing what she had done to their friend Eric in the stables, "no questions asked". His heart bled, his chest tightened.

Without thinking, he drew her into his arms.

"Don't," she protested feebly. But she made no move to disentangle herself, as if the embrace was welcome.

"Please, Raven. Just let me hold you." He needed it, as much as she did. He needed to know he was doing what little he could to help her; he needed to know he was not the heartless bastard he'd been with her. "I'm sorry. I'm so sorry. For everything you've been through, for not immediately understanding what was happening, for what I told you the other day, for the way I spoke to you."

For taking the men's word without knowing the reality of the situation. For thinking her a whore, and talking to her accordingly. For being angry with her. For threatening her. For so many things.

"I'm so sorry."

"It's all right. None of it is your fault, and you could not have guessed."

That did not make it much better. He should have seen that something was not right the moment she had leapt to Elena's defense that day in the bailey. Now he understood why seeing what she thought was an assault would have traumatized her.

His hold around her tightened. Her confession had cost her, and it deserved one from him in return. Matthew knew just what to tell her. She'd confided something no one knew, something personal and painful, she had opened up to him.

He would do just the same.

"I was a virgin before you made a man out of me that day in

the solar," he whispered, his mouth at her temple. "You're the first person I have told as much. No one knows about it, not even Connor. Everyone assumes I've had more lovers than I can count. But the truth is, I'd never lain with a woman before that day."

He felt her stiffen against him, not quite the reaction he'd expected, and she drew back to look at him. "You? A virgin?"

Branwen was incredulous. A man as well-favored as Matthew, a virgin? He was virility personified. She'd been so sure he'd bedded scores of women only too eager to be led astray! And she was being told he had never had a lover.

He shrugged, as if embarrassed by the admission, and refused to meet her eye. "It was the only way. I was no innocent, don't get me wrong. I had pleasured women and allowed them to pleasure me in turn, but I'd never ..." He pursed his lips but she understood what he meant. He had never entered a woman's body.

"Why not?" She hated to pry, but she had to know. It seemed too incredible that a man like him had not been with a woman before two weeks ago. There had to be a reason. When he spoke, his answer confirmed her impression.

"I knew that, as an inexperienced lover, I would find it impossible to keep myself from spilling inside a woman, and the last thing I wanted was to leave bastards in my wake. There are enough of them in the world."

"Yes." Branwen didn't quite know what to say.

"The best way not to tempt fate was to not possess anyone. And it seems I was right to be wary of my ability to control myself or doubt my skill at pleasing the woman in my arms," he said with a grimace. "That day in the solar I lasted as long as an untried youth, I was as desperate for release as a man half my age, and I did nothing to bring you pleasure."

He sounded so disgusted with himself Branwen couldn't bear it.

"You have nothing to be ashamed of. Nothing of what happened is your fault. You know now about my inability to feel pleasure." She blushed, but she was determined to be honest. Her embarrassment didn't count, she needed to reassure him. "And you didn't last because I ... I did everything I could to precipitate your pleasure. It was all *my* fault, not yours"

Having had so many men, she knew all about what made them unable to last any longer than necessary. Usually, she did so because she wanted the ordeal to be over as quickly as possible, but with Matthew it had been different. She had wanted to put an end to it because she had started to feel sensations she didn't want to feel.

And she had succeeded in spectacular fashion.

He'd been hurtled headlong into his climax. Now she understood why he'd been so primed, why his release had been so explosive. It had been his first time. All his life he had refrained from making love to women because he didn't want to spill his seed inside them and risk fathering children he would never see grow.

And she had forced him to do just that. She had made him take her, made him come in the way most suited to her.

She collapsed onto the stool behind her as realisation hit. Even if, admittedly, she had not hurt Matthew in the process, she was no better than Bryn, who had taken her innocence before she was ready, who'd thought it his right to decide when and where she became aware of what transpired between men and women.

"My God. I'm so sorry. I had no idea. And I forced you to ... I'm not better than—"

"No, it was nothing like that, and you know it!" Matthew cut in, falling to his knees in front of her. "I won't let you think such a thing. You didn't use force, you didn't hurt me, you didn't even take anything I didn't want to give. It was nothing like what happened to you with that bastard, do you hear? I could have said no and you would have heeded my refusal. I could have lifted you off my lap in the blink of an eye if I'd wanted to. But I didn't. I wanted you, more than anything I'd ever wanted in my life, more than my next breath. If you hadn't taken me, I believe I would have taken you there against the wall, and to hell with everything."

There was no doubting his sincerity. He meant it absolutely. For a reason she couldn't explain, he would have done with her what he had refused to do with other women.

"Why?" she asked, staring at him straight in the eye.

He shook his head slowly, as if he didn't have the answer to that question and regretted not being able to answer. "I don't know why, in the same way that I'm not sure you know why you wanted me so badly you gifted me with what so many men have taken by force."

How had he guessed that he had been the first man she had ever felt desire for? That their lovemaking had been the first time she had ever initiated such intimacy? Though she was no virgin, like he had been, in her heart he'd been her first lover, he had given her the first time she wished she'd had.

"You're right," she said slowly. "It's inexplicable."

"But undeniable."

Matthew could only agree. There was something between them, had been from the start. They could both see it. As to what they could do with it, that was not so easy to decide.

While he was pondering what to say next, a woman entered the cottage without knocking, and started talking in Welsh. It was obvious she felt at home and did not expect anyone other than Branwen to be inside. Matthew had no idea what she was saying but she stopped abruptly when she saw him kneeling at Branwen's feet.

Slowly, even if was too late to pretend he had not been in such an intimate position, he stood back up.

"Mam, this is Matthew," Branwen said in Welsh, articulating for his benefit.

Mam? Though he'd never heard the word before, it was not hard to guess it was what Welsh people called their mother. But with her fair complexion and blue eyes, the woman looked nothing like Branwen, even if she seemed just about old enough to have given birth to her. It seemed he was not the only one who'd been raised by someone who wasn't his birth mother.

How odd. He had just been thinking that her confession had stirred his protective instinct. Now he was finding out that they had more in common than he had supposed. Added to the attraction he already felt, it was making it harder and harder to keep his distance from her.

He hadn't understood at the time what had drawn her to him, but he knew now what would keep him enthralled.

The two women started a rapid exchange, one he could not follow and likely had no business to overhear. Doing his best to appear as if he wasn't listening, he went to stir the fire embers. The older woman was looking at him strangely, as if trying to make sense of him. After a while she nodded and disappeared through the door again, taking her daughter with her. He guessed she would ask Branwen who he was as soon as they were out of earshot.

He went to the window and took a moment to observe the interior of the cottage. It was clean and well looked after, but very sparsely furnished. This was not the abode of a rich woman. He'd already remarked that Branwen's clothes, though always clean, had been darned a few times, and that her frame was slender, almost to the point of thinness. He looked at the basket full of sorry-looking apples. The fruit looked almost rotten. Was she eating enough? Did she have all the wood she needed to keep warm at night? What protection did she have against intruders? The contrast between them was suddenly glaring. At Esgyrn Castle, not only did he have plenty to eat, but he also had access to luxury items such as the sugared almonds he favored; he was never cold or in any danger.

He would have to make sure Branwen was well-fed, warm, and protected.

After what she'd revealed, she needed to feel secure more than any other woman he knew. A fierce guard dog would be a start. A litter had been born at Esgyrn Castle a few months back to one of Connor's wolfhounds. Perhaps a pup could be spared. He would speak to his brother without delay, because he couldn't bear to think of Branwen all alone in her cottage, an easy prey to the predatory men lurking around.

A moment later, she was back. She looked shy, as if not quite sure how to resume the conversation, which was little wonder given what they had been discussing when they'd been interrupted. He could not help but admire her fortitude. After all she had endured, she could have been forgiven for staying away from him.

"That was Carys, my ... well, the woman I consider as my mother. She raised my sister and me when our mother died. I was ten then." So he'd guessed correctly, the two women were not related by blood. "She came to get her back. They live together at the other end of the village, even if we often spend the day together."

He coughed, remembering he'd been on his knees in front of Branwen when the woman had entered the hut. "I hope it wasn't a problem for her to see me kneeling before you?" he asked, not wanting to place her in an uncomfortable position.

At best, the woman would have thought he had just been

pleasuring her daughter intimately, at worst, that he was one of the men taking advantage of her. *If* Branwen had told a woman who was as good as her mother about what she had gone through as a young girl and was still going through, that was. He would not be surprised if she'd kept her ordeal and the direness of her situation from her, in order to spare her from pain.

Branwen flushed a delightful color. "Don't worry about her. I'm a grown woman now, so she didn't ask any questions. I can do what I want with my life."

Except she couldn't. That was the whole problem.

Silence stretched between them. The sun had already started its decent toward the horizon.

"Matthew ... I would ask something of you but I dare not."

"Ask me." He would not have her hesitant with him, and if he could atone in any way for what he had done to her, he would. "Anything."

"I would like you to stay with me tonight. Of course, if you have somewhere else you have to be, I'll understand," she added hurriedly, as if she regretted her request, or thought she was overstepping the mark.

But it did not take Matthew long to agree. Hadn't he been thinking just a moment ago that he wanted her to be safe? Yes, he had. He was not going anywhere. With him around, at least tonight, nothing would happen to her.

He took her hand. "Of course. I will stay."

Chapter Seven

Branwen woke up nose to nose with a man, something that had never happened in her life. Her hazy mind took a moment to remember who the man was and what he was doing in her bed. When it finally did, it was too late. The scream had already left her throat.

"What the—"

Cursing, Matthew bolted to his feet and darted to the scabbard he'd placed on the table the previous evening. Before Branwen had time to recover from the shock of waking up in a man's arms for the first time in her life, she was staring at a warrior ready to fight. Eyes ablaze, hair in disarray, sword drawn, he was magnificent.

He was also half naked—and hard.

Branwen swallowed. She knew men woke up in such a state, so this was likely not caused by their proximity during the night, but it did not seem to make much difference to the heat invading her body. Everything that was feminine within her seemed to respond to the proof of his virility. Dear God, but this man was making her feel things she'd always thought herself incapable of.

"Are you all right?" he asked, eyes glued to the door, as if he expected an enemy to burst in at any moment. "What did you hear? What's happening?"

"Nothing, I'm sorry," she croaked, trying to settle the beating of her heart, something made rather difficult by the sight in front of her. "Only, I saw you in my bed when I opened my eyes, and for a moment I thought ... I didn't know who you were. I panicked."

He lowered his weapon and nodded, muscles relaxing. "I see. Of course. It is understandable."

The sword was placed back in its sheath without comment. Only then did he seem to realize the sight he was presenting with his naked chest and his shaft tenting his braies. He coughed and turned around on the pretext of helping himself to some ale from the pitcher on the table. Branwen was grateful for the intention.

While he drank, she did her best to restore her composure. Her cheeks were burning and her throat was dry. After a while, she averted her eyes, because his back was no less alluring than his chest, if in a different way. Strong muscles bracketed his spine, tapering his trim waist to come kiss the perfect, tight buttocks hidden under his braies. The simple act of lifting the cup to his lips caused his bicep to bulge and her insides to melt in answer.

By all that was holy, how could such a man exist, never mind be in her home, half naked, after having spent the night in her bed? And how could she not lust after him? She had no idea. Perhaps she should simply stop fighting temptation and accept what was blossoming inside her. It felt good, soothing, like gentle rain falling over a scorched landscape, nothing spectacular, but still strong enough to be felt, and welcome. Could it be enough to restore life to it, make it whole again? She hadn't felt alive for so long, or so it seemed, that she didn't know.

In just a few days, Matthew Hunter had made her see that perhaps all hope was not lost. She might be able to heal one day, in the same way a burned landscape could become lush again.

"Could you ..." she started, her voice reduced to a whisper. What did she want to ask? She wasn't sure. "Could you pour me a cup as well, please?"

"Of course."

Matthew handed a cup full of ale to Branwen, who refused to meet his eye when she accepted it.

Was she ashamed of having woken him up with a start, or as affected by their proximity as he was? Both explanations seemed possible. He'd never slept next to a woman before, so perhaps the experience was new for her as well. The scream that had split his ear upon waking up certainly seemed to suggest so. After what she had told him about her life, he doubted she held men in high esteem, and the ones who came to her certainly didn't come to sleep, so it stood to reason she had never spent the night next to anyone.

Perhaps it had been for the best she'd awoken him so abruptly, for who knew what he would have done if he'd found himself with a sweet-smelling, warm, alluring woman next to him when his mind was still prey to the mists of sleep? It would have appeared like a dream. He might have reached out for her, his hand might have landed on her breast. He had only suckled her before, not caressed her, but he knew they would feel perfect in his hand, soft and pert at the same time. The pointy tip would have teased his palm and before he knew it, he would have squeezed and rubbed, before rolling her under him and—

No! he chided himself. He could not think like that. His erection had finally gone down, he could not resurrect it now with such lewd thoughts. With his body under control, they might be able to have a sensible conversation. After what she had endured, what she was enduring still, Branwen was the last woman he could afford to frighten with the proof of his lust.

"Does your sister visit you often then?" he asked, seizing the first subject that came to mind.

"Yes, at least once a week. Her name is Eirwen," she said almost shyly, as if she had not mentioned her sister to many people and wasn't sure how to talk about her. He felt honored by this mark of trust and, to hide his emotion, decided to tease her.

"Ah. Eir*wen*. So 'white' something, but what? Coal? Pepper? You never know what goes through the mind of you Welsh people."

To his relief, she laughed, easing some of the tension in the cottage. "No. As Welsh names go, hers is quite sensible. It means 'white snow'."

"Yes. Very sensible." He pursed his lips. "As fancy, poetic names go, that is. We are still a far cry from Mary or Elizabeth, I would say."

She made a dismissive gesture with her hand. "Yes, but my parents would never have given us such English names, in the same way that yours would not have called you Iorwerth or Maredudd."

Matthew gave a mock shiver intended to relax her further. After the difficult conversation they'd had the day before, he didn't want to leave her to mull over her dreadful past and the vile men populating it when he left, as he must soon. Connor would be waiting for him at Esgyrn Castle, wondering why he'd spent the night away from the place for the first time since they'd arrived.

But he knew he would have difficulty thinking about anything else for the days to come. Branwen's confession had shaken him to his core. For now, though, he would behave as bravely as she was, and pretend her life was normal.

"Thank the Lord they didn't call me that, for who's ever heard of a man not able to pronounce his name properly?"

Branwen could not believe this conversation. Who would have thought dour Matthew Hunter could be so understanding and gentle? She had kept her story a secret, not only because she was ashamed, though she certainly was, but because she had not thought anyone could believe her. They would assume she was merely trying to justify her scandalous behavior and hide a lustful nature. But against all odds the forbidding Englishman had listened to her, been outraged on her behalf, and agreed to stay the night with her. Now, he was even making her laugh. It was perfect, and she wasn't sure she wanted him to leave. Ever.

Pushing such thoughts out of her mind, she asked. "Your parents must have wanted the best for you, to give you such an easy name to pronounce."

Branwen regretted the comment the moment the words passed her lips. She had meant it as a jest, but Matthew's face, so open a moment ago, closed up. The topic of his parents was obviously a painful one. For a moment he didn't say anything, instead helping himself to a second cup of ale.

"You must know I'm not Connor's real brother?" he said eventually, running a hand through his hair.

Yes. Esyllt had told her as much a few months ago. "You're his milk brother."

"Aye, and a bastard."

She flinched, as much at his harsh word as the bitterness in his voice. "I'm sorry," she said inadequately.

"Don't be sorry. It's not your fault."

No, it wasn't, but she should have guessed it would be a sensitive topic. She of all people knew what dark secrets sometimes lurked in people's pasts.

"Do you want to tell me about it?"

Damnation, where had that question come from? Her mind

had really been addled by the proximity of his naked chest. She'd just seen that the topic of his parents was a sensitive one. Why would he want to share it, with her or anyone?

But to her surprise and relief, he joined her back on the pallet and started to talk.

"My mother, Rose, was a maid at Sheridan Manor. She birthed me the day before Connor was born, which was why she was chosen to feed him. Despite our difference in stations, the two of us grew up to be as close as real brothers can be."

Yes. This Branwen knew as well. Her friend had made no secret of the bond between the two men, and the protectiveness of her brother-in-law toward her husband. She had seen the proof of it herself. Matthew would die for Connor without the least hesitation. "Esyllt told me as much."

"When I was six, my mother died of a fever. I don't know what would have happened to me if Connor had not made his parents raise me. Though I was only the bastard son of their maid, they fostered me as they would have the son of a noble family. I will always be grateful to them for the opportunity they gave me, for I never had any family who could have taken me in."

"Your father ..." Her voice trailed, but Matthew didn't seem to take offense. Perhaps after what she had confided in him the day before, he thought no topic was too sensitive between them. It certainly felt that way.

"I have never known who my father was, only that he never married my mother or bothered to find out what had happened to her, or me. I would hate him if I knew who he was, but I don't even have that luxury." He clenched his jaw. "I often wish I could meet him just so I could plant my fist in his face."

That had to be the saddest thing Branwen had ever heard, and she was no stranger to misery.

"I'm—" He stopped her by throwing her a glance that might have passed for amused had they been discussing something less serious. She almost smiled back. "Well, forgive me, I know none of this is my fault, but I *am* sorry all the same. It must be hard."

He took her hand in his and gave it a comforting squeeze. "It is. Especially that I am under no illusions. He was probably a visiting noble who thought he could use the servants to empty his aching balls whenever the need—"

Matthew stopped and stared at Branwen in horror. How could he have said something like that? How could he have been so crude when he knew dozens of men had used her for precisely that purpose, when she was in constant danger of ending up like his mother, raising a bastard child imposed on her? Never had he felt worse in his life.

"I'm sorry. Please forgive me. I'm a fool, I don't know why I said that," he said, lifting the hand he was still holding and kissing each of her fingers in turn. How could he make amends for his thoughtlessness?

"You said it because it's true," she whispered, as if taken aback by the gesture. Nevertheless, she didn't take her hand away, for which he was grateful. Holding her felt good. "We both know there are too many men like this."

Yes, they did, but the difference was, she had learned it the hard way and suffered every day because of it. He should never have said anything that would remind her of her ordeal.

"Is that why you don't bed women, why you don't want to father illegitimate children?"

The question was blunt, and stirred painful emotions within him, but he welcomed it because it meant that she had by some miracle forgiven him for his awful lapse in judgment. Though he wasn't sure he deserved her generosity, he was comforted by the notion.

"Yes, that's why I was a virgin, why I was determined not to bed a woman until I married." He had told her the day before he didn't want to be responsible for a little boy or girl growing up without a father, but not the reason why. Now was the time. "I wanted to be sure my children were legitimate, and grew up with their father. I was tempted, of course, many times, but every time I wanted to allow my urges to take over, I could not. Everything within me froze and I could not go through with it. A man cannot perform if his body doesn't cooperate."

She reddened, no doubt remembering that it had not happened like that between them. *She* had taken the initiative, before he could think the better of it, and had not given him much choice. True, as he'd said, he could have lifted her off his lap, but by then it had been too late. His body, so often unresponsive when in a woman's arms, had betrayed him. It had done more than cooperate, it had leapt at the chance to take what it had craved all these years.

"I'm sorry I—"

"I'm not sorry you did. I told you. I would have burst if you had not taken me." Though he didn't say it, he was honored she would have wanted to take him in the first place. To know that she had trusted him enough to want to see how it would feel to take a man for once, as opposed to being taken against her will.

"If it eases your mind, you can be assured our encounter will not bear fruit," Branwen said shyly.

Yes, it should ease his mind, but oddly it brought a lump to his chest. "You mean that you've bled since?" It had only been a few days, but it was possible she already knew she was not with child.

"No, not yet." The color on her cheeks reached alarming proportions, discussing such intimate details.

"Then how can you be sure?"

"I visit a healer regularly, and take herbs that prevent conception. I can't afford not to. The risk of falling with child is too great, considering ..." Yes. Considering she was bedded by every randy goat that crossed her path. He bunched his fists, remembering how he had accused her of being in a position to have a child fathered by a man whose identity she wouldn't know. He swore never to speak like this to a woman ever again. "As much as I love children and wish to have my own babes one day, just like you, I refuse to have one when I know I will not be able to offer them the safety of a family."

He nodded. Of course she would take herbs. It made sense that she would do what she could to preserve what little choice she had. She could not stop the men from coming to her but she could ensure she did not bear their bastards. God on the cross, he wished he could geld each and every one of the ones who had dared place a hand on her.

"Is that why you don't want to be around children?" he asked softly.

To think he had mocked her for it, when she was only trying to spare herself the pain of seeing what she thought she could never have.

"Yes. 'Tis just too painful, because I know this joy is not for me."

The expression of sorrow on her face was a knife to the gut. Would there be no end to his shame?

"Please, Branwen. Though I know I do not deserve it, I ask for your forgiveness for what I said the day Esyllt gave birth. I behaved like the bastard I am. It was cruel and—"

"You're forgiven," she cut in. "After all you'd heard and seen about me, you could not have thought any different. You had seen a man come out of my cottage, a man who'd told you ... what I'd done to him."

Yes, the blasted Englishman had boasted about using her talented mouth. "I should have throttled him for what he made you do." If the man had the gall to come knocking at her door now, he would gut him before a word of protest could pass his lips.

"He didn't make me, exactly. More often than not, I am the one who suggests it." She flushed at the admission, as if fearing he would think it was through personal preference. He did not, because he knew none of this was her choice. "It's less painful than to have men actually take me and it reduces the chances of conceiving. I cannot bear the idea of having a son who would grow up a bastard and never know who his father was." She stared at him, knowing he would understand the pain that could cause. "Or a daughter who would only grow up to be used like I am."

"Oh, sweet." His heart broke, and he almost drew her into his arms. "This would never happen to a child of yours. You're too strong. You would love your son as fiercely as my mother loved me, and you would protect your daughter like you protected Eirwen. And perhaps ... perhaps one day there will be a man by your side to help take care of the children you secretly crave?"

"I think not." She gave a sad smile, resigned to her fate. "For what man would have a child with me, when they could not be sure who the father was? When they knew I'd been possessed by dozens of men? When they thought a child of mine could end up like my sister, whom everyone here pities or mocks? That man would have to be a fool."

I'm no fool, Matthew thought. *And I would have a child with this woman.*

He started. Where had that thought come from? He'd never considered having children, at least not until he was safely married and certain their legitimacy could not be put in question. At the back of his mind he knew he wanted children, just like any man, but because he didn't feel ready to take a wife yet, he had not given the possibility any real thought.

Connor had on occasion introduced him to ladies of modest rank, hinting that a union between them would be acceptable to their fathers, who were of the opinion that his connection to the Hunter family was as valuable as any real title would have been. He was, for all intents and purposes, Lord Sheridan's only brother, and that was worth something.

Matthew had always been uncomfortable with the idea of marrying one of those ladies, however, because say what he might, he did not belong to the same world as his nobly born brother, and he would never be at ease amongst people who would make him feel the difference between them in subtle and no-so-subtle ways.

He'd never dared tell Connor as much, because he didn't want to appear ungrateful and his brother's intentions were laudable. Instead, he'd always found real or imaginary faults with the women to justify his refusal to consider proposing to them.

To give him his due, Connor had stopped pushing for such a union since he'd married Esyllt more than a year ago. Perhaps he now thought that there could, and should, be more to marriage than mere convenience. Matthew was relieved, because he would never have been happy as the husband of a lady, even one of modest rank. He would always have felt at a disadvantage, not a comfortable position for a man. He wanted to be chosen on his own merit, not because he'd been lucky to be raised by a powerful lord.

His birth hadn't been planned. His father hadn't wanted him, his mother hadn't chosen to have him. In all probability he had been imposed on her, and even if she had loved him, he didn't want to spend the rest of his life feeling he had been imposed on anyone, much less his wife.

But with a simple villager who'd fallen for the man he was, not the lord's brother, there would be no danger of this happening. He would not feel like a fraud. A simple villager like the one standing in front of him, a beautiful, brave woman who had made a man out of him.

Dear God, this was all turning into such a mess.

"My life is such a mess," Branwen said, echoing his thoughts. "If I didn't have Eirwen I often think I would ..."

Matthew blinked when her voice trailed. What was she saying? Not what he was thinking, surely? She was not considering ending her own life?

"I forbid you to think like that, do you hear me? You are the bravest, most selfless woman I have ever met," he said fiercely, taking her by the shoulders. "I will not have you—"

A knock on the door interrupted him, quickly followed by a man's voice, speaking in Welsh. He felt Branwen stiffen under his palms and she shook her head, indicating he should not respond, and pretend she was out. Yes. Good idea. He was not ready to put an end to the moment they were sharing either. When no one answered, the banging resumed, betraying the man's impatience.

"Branwen, I know you're in there." Matthew could not be sure that was what the man had said, but it had to be something to that effect. A kick on the door was heard next, then what he imagined to be a curse.

He didn't stop to think.

He sprang to his feet, sword at the ready. The bastard had to be one of those men who thought Branwen was only here to satisfy his needs. There was no other explanation. A friend, or even a simple visitor would not be trying to break down the door to see her. Well, he would regret choosing today of all days to come to her, and Matthew would enjoy unleashing the powerlessness he'd felt after hearing Branwen's story. Much better to pummel a pathetic weasel to the ground than go mad with frustration.

Quick as a flash, he unbolted the door, and fell onto the unsuspecting intruder. He had the blade of his sword pressing against the side of his neck before the man had time to understand what was happening. His eyes widened with fear and Matthew could not resist nicking at the flesh, and letting the man feel his blood trickle down his neck. Serves him right for thinking he could barge in Branwen's home at dawn, demanding to be serviced. Only the fact that she could see them prevented him from inflicting a much more gruesome injury, one that would ensure this sad excuse for a man could not bother any woman ever again.

"Whether Branwen is here or not is of no interest to you, do you hear, you bastard?" he growled, his nose a mere inch from the man's temple. "Go and jerk yourself off in the forest if you need release. You will never touch a hair on her head ever again, or I guarantee it will be the last thing you do."

It was obvious the man didn't understand the English words. Nevertheless, he could not mistake the intent. He was to leave Branwen alone.

There was a garbled sound Matthew did not even try to interpret. He was too far gone in anger. Up until that day he would not have thought he was a vicious man, but he was starting to think differently. He wanted to see the man squirm and regret ever laying eyes on the woman he'd taken under his protection.

"Or perhaps *I* should see to your needs, see how you like that," he purred, grabbing him by the crotch and giving a cruel squeeze. "Word of warning, I might not be as gentle as you wish."

A word that he assumed to be a plea left the man's lips.

"Wait, Matthew!" he heard Branwen cry from behind him. "It's not what you think, he's not one of the ... He's only the owner of the cottage."

The owner of the cottage? This stopped Matthew in his tracks.

It seemed he'd been wrong and the man was not after sexual gratification. Still, the realization failed to make him regret his actions because there had been no mistaking the aggression in the man's voice. He'd pounded at her door like a man possessed and would have forced his way into the hut had Matthew not stopped him. Whether he'd been here to bed Branwen or not, it was clear he could not be trusted not to hurt her.

Nevertheless, in view of what he'd been told, he had no choice but to release him. The man grunted in relief, and dabbed at his neck slowly. He whimpered when he found his hand wet with blood. Not sorry in the least, Matthew came to stand behind Branwen. With his bare chest and his hair in disarray, he guessed he would appear like her lover, fresh from her bed. Well, all the better to give him some legitimacy for defending her. If the Welshman thought the two of them were involved, he might think twice about bothering her. An Englishman in possession of a sword and a destrier was not someone to be dismissed lightly.

Before he could think, Matthew placed a hand on the small of Branwen's back, the gesture signaling without doubt that she was under his protection.

"What does he want, then?" he growled. Damn it all, if only he could understand what was going on. Now that he lived here, he would really have to learn the people's language. The alternative was dying of frustration.

"He's come to collect what I owe him for this month but ..."

She didn't finish the sentence but there was no need. This

month she didn't have what she owed the man, whatever that was. It didn't surprise him. Hadn't he remarked the day before that she didn't appear to have enough to live in comfort? It would have been extraordinary if she'd had anything to spare for anyone.

It was obvious from the look in the man's eyes, however, that he was not too worried about Branwen's lack of funds. In a moment he would offer her a way of acquitting herself of the debt in a manner that did not involve money. The blood in Matthew's veins heated up again and the hand at the small of Branwen's back snaked around her waist to draw her closer. The possessiveness of the gesture was not lost on the man, who took a step back, as if remembering this could end badly for him.

Yes, very wise.

Matthew turned to look at Branwen. "Tell him to take this, and not to come back to see you again before the beginning of next year," he said, articulating each word carefully. "There should be enough in here to satisfy him until then at least."

As he spoke, he extracted two gold coins from the purse he always carried at his belt and threw them to the Welshman who stared at them in stupefaction. In all probability, it was more money than he'd ever held in his life. Well, he was welcome to it. Matthew would have paid a king's ransom to keep Branwen safe.

"No, you cannot!" she started to protest.

"I already have. This is not just for you. Connor will not countenance to have any of his tenants being harassed thus. He put me in charge of the smooth running of the estate. That's what this money's for." He nodded to his purse, which still contained three times the amount he'd given the man. "Fret not, he will give me the money as soon as I get back to the castle."

Of course, there was no such arrangement and his brother would not even hear about the sum he'd supposedly spent to ensure Branwen spent a year free of worry, but Matthew had to say something because he could tell she was uncomfortable with accepting charity. He didn't like to put her ill at ease, and he wanted to preserve her pride as much as possible, but the priority was her safety and well-being. There was no way he could allow the man to have any excuse to demand her favors, today or ever.

The Welshman needed to be told in no uncertain terms he had better not bother her ever again. If she surrendered once, he would only be back for more. The idea was unbearable.

When she hesitated, he added, "Tell him that you are now under the protection of Lord Sheridan, as is everyone in the village." *And mine.* He didn't add the words but he hoped she could see them in his eyes. "Make sure he gets it into his thick head that if he has any grievances, he should bring them to him."

Her voice trembling, Branwen translated his words to the man, who shook his head vehemently, as if to say he didn't have any complaints. Matthew was not so easily appeased by this apparent surrender. The bastard had definitely hoped for an opportunity to abuse his power. What would have happened if Branwen had not asked him to spend the night in her cottage didn't bear thinking about.

"Thank you," Branwen sounded so relieved he could not help but tighten his hold around her. "He says he will not be back before next spring."

"Oh, but he will. He will be back before the end of the week to see to the hole at the back of the roof. If this really is his cottage, then it is his responsibility to see that it is in good repair." The man would not get away with shirking his duty as easily.

Branwen's lovely eyes went as round as coins, and almost as shiny. "You saw that?"

"Of course. It's a disgrace. He had better get it fixed before I mention it to Lord Sheridan, who will not be as lenient as I am."

As soon as she had translated his words, he dragged the dishonorable owner to the back of the hut, and pointed at the damaged roof menacingly. The man nodded so much Matthew feared his neck might break under the strain.

"*Diolch.*"

Though he was loath to thank the man for promising to do something that should have been done weeks ago, it was a way of ending the conversation and making him understand he assumed the repairs would be done without further intervention on his part. For good measure, Matthew planted his sword into the ground, the message clear. As long as the man held his end of the bargain, he would be safe.

After one last word to Branwen, the man left.

"He said he would be back in two days' time."

"Good." He stayed in front of her a long time, then shivered when he remembered he was still bare-chested. Up until then, too enraged by the man's attitude, he had not felt the cold. "I think I will go and get dressed now. I don't want to end up as the next English skeleton in a ditch when I perish from cold."

Branwen's lips quivered, making it impossible for him not to think about kissing her. He ran back inside the cottage to find his undershirt and tunic before he could do that.

As soon as Matthew had disappeared from view, Branwen collapsed on the bench behind her.

Thank God he'd been there.

Daffydd had been about to demand she service him to compensate for her inability to pay what she owed him; she had seen the intention in his eyes. She had seen that look too many times to doubt it. The mere idea had sent her stomach roiling. Had Matthew not intervened, she would have found herself in an impossible situation, because there was no way she would have agreed to lie with him. It would only have made him think that from now on he could use her as his whore, as well as collect the rent she owed him.

Now she was safe from Daffydd's advances, and guaranteed to keep a home for almost a year. Though she wasn't sure she believed the story of Connor being the one behind this generosity, she had been too weak to refuse Matthew's help. What alternative did she have?

He reappeared a moment later, splendid with his velvet tunic and scabbard around his trim waist. The difference in status between them struck her anew. Here was a knight in all his splendor, not a poor villager. Because she had been friends with Esyllt all her life, and used to going to Castell Esgyrn, she had never thought twice of being in the presence of noble people. But with him ... Or perhaps it had nothing to do with his clothes, and more to do with his attitude toward her, or the fact that she had confided in him, or that they had kissed, and made love.

Everything was different with him.

"I'll be going now. Connor will be wondering where I am." He glanced in the direction of Esgyrn Castle. "Will you be all right on your own?"

A lump rose in her throat, because suddenly she wasn't sure she was ready to see him go. "I have lived alone for years," she forced herself to answer.

"Yes." And they both knew what kind of life she'd had. He didn't need to say more.

"Thank you, Matthew. For ... everything."

For listening to me, for not judging, for staying with me last night, for defending me against Daffydd, for forgiving what I did to you, when I took your virginity.

The list was endless.

Matthew moved. At first Branwen thought he was going to

go to the stallion waiting for him, but he stopped in front of her instead and drew her to him. For a moment it looked as if he was about to kiss her. He was cradling the back of her neck in his palms, with his thumbs resting on her cheeks. There was so much tenderness in the gesture that she felt tears spring to her eyes. What was he doing to her? Wasn't he supposed to be scathing, detached, arrogant, forbidding, cruel—anything but understanding and kind?

"Thank you for trusting me with your story," he said, his voice thick with emotion. "And I am sorry for having been such a blind idiot. I should have seen something was not right."

"It's not your fault. Considering what you heard about me and what you saw, you couldn't have—"

"I could. But it won't happen again. I promise."

She could only nod and he finally released her. Without a word he walked over to his stallion, who'd spent the night tethered to the old beech. She watched while he got him ready with swift, efficient gestures. There was something preying on her mind, but she wasn't sure how to broach the topic. Once he'd tightened the girth on the saddle, she found the courage to speak out.

"There is something I would ask before you leave."

He turned to face her, eyes ablaze. "Of course. Anything."

"What did you mean that day by the lake when you asked me who had sent me to you?"

She had tried to puzzle it out since then, without coming up with a satisfactory explanation. Now was as good a time as any to ask him. To her surprise, he shuffled on his feet, and lowered his gaze to the ground. If she'd not known him for a confident, powerful knight, she would have thought he was embarrassed. Eventually, he answered, his voice low.

"I feared when I first met you that you had been sent to me by a Welsh rebel."

Branwen received the full impact of the insult like a blow to the chest. "You mean ... someone like Gruffydd? You thought I'd kissed you because I was trying to lure you in, bring you to a man who wanted you dead because you're English?"

The look on his face was enough to tell her that yes, he had thought that. Branwen was both horrified and outraged and she didn't try to hide it. He'd thought her in league with a murderer, thought her capable of sending a man to his death.

It was unbearable.

"I'm sorry. But after what had happened to Connor, I had to be careful. I couldn't understand why you'd acted the way you did. Kissing me, making love to me without me even trying to seduce you. It made no sense to me. We were strangers and we were supposed to be enemies." He took her hands in his, his face a mask of contrition. "Now that I know you, and your story, I am sorrier than I can say for doubting your motives. I know you could never have done anything like that. Only, I couldn't understand why you would want to be with an Englishman you didn't know. It was the only explanation I could think of. I'm a suspicious man by nature and had to guard myself and my family by necessity."

Her fury dissipated as quickly as it had come, because she could see it hadn't been personal. As he'd said, only a few months ago his brother had been the victim of a similar plot, and had been captured because his wife had been the one helping the rebels. Esyllt had been blackmailed, of course, but it went to show that women could all too easily be used as tools to get to the despised invaders. Why would she not be one such woman? Matthew would have been a fool to trust an unknown Welsh woman throwing herself at him.

"And now, what do you think?" Though she thought she already knew the answer, she needed to hear it from his lips.

"Now I understand that I am the luckiest man in all the

world. The only man you have ever wanted and whom you trusted with your story. Now I know I have nothing to fear from you and your motives were pure as snow. Or whatever other dark substance you mad Welsh people would consider pure."

Tears welled in Branwen's eyes at the same time as laughter burst through her lips. The silly man! How dare he mock her in that moment. Would she ever meet another man like him? Perhaps. Would she want him as much as she wanted this one? It was doubtful.

Matthew lifted the hands he was still holding and kissed them gently.

"Will you forgive me, Raven, for thinking the worst of you?"

"You didn't. And you don't need my forgiveness for being cautious."

It was her turn to lift his hands to her lips and place a kiss on each. She watched as his eyes darkened and she realized she didn't want him to leave. Dare she ask him to stay another night?

Before she could say anything, he took a step back.

"I will be back three days hence to see if the roof has been repaired," he said, before vaulting on top of his stallion.

Branwen nodded again, a small smile tugging at her lips despite her wretchedness. Heaven help Daffydd if he didn't keep his promise.

∽

Matthew stormed to the barbican, his mood as black as it had ever been. On the ride back to Esgyrn Castle he had played his conversation with Branwen again and again in his mind, in every painful detail, and he was now itching for a fight. He hadn't been able to use the cottage owner to ease his frustration, but the two men guarding the gate might provide a satisfactory outlet for his anger, because he had not forgotten a word of their exchange either.

"My lo—"

"How many times did she come?" he growled, backing them both into a corner. He felt like a savage dog about to rip a coney to pieces.

"I b-beg your p-pardon?" Owen stammered, looking at his friend with wild eyes. They clearly both feared they would end up with his sword through the gut, an all too likely possibility at the moment, Matthew had to admit. He was in a rare state.

"Branwen, the Welsh girl you told me about the other day. The one you took turns with." Christ almighty, imagining Branwen alone with the two of them was enough to make him want to retch. "You said you labored over her all night, so how many times did she come? Five? Ten times?"

"Well ..." The men looked at one another uncertainly.

"How many times?" he snarled, placing himself in front of them. "Think. Did she moan? Did she say anything?"

He remembered their vile boasting.

Did she utter a word of protest?

No, he now knew she wouldn't have, and why. She hadn't protested, wary of what the two burly men would do if she refused them when they were aroused. Facing one man's retribution was daunting enough for a slight woman, two was inconceivable. So she had waited for it to be over, praying to get out of the ordeal unscathed, just as she did every time. It had been as it always was. Owen and Thomas had come to her, drawn by her reputation of willingness, and she had been too petrified to say anything, too desperate not to provoke their ire to offer any resistance. Dear God, the notion of all she'd had to endure was unbearable.

The two friends looked at one another as if realizing only now that her behavior had been odd. Too aroused to think overmuch or see the clues, they had genuinely thought her a willing participant, he could tell.

Well, he would make sure they were left in no doubt about what had really happened.

"Who initiated it? You said she didn't say no. But did you go to her or did she come to you?"

"We did," Thomas admitted slowly. "Edgar had told us she'd ridden him like a wild thing the week before, so we thought we'd try our luck as well. What harm could it do? And just like we'd hoped, she didn't refuse."

It was all clear as crystal. Branwen was trapped in a hell of her own making. The more men she was unable to refuse, the more her reputation as a willing woman grew. Men were starting to flock to her, two by two. Where would it stop? This was becoming dangerous and he had to put an end to it immediately.

"Listen to me, and listen well," he told the two guards, making sure to appear every inch Lord Sheridan's powerful brother. "You are not to go to her ever again, and if she visits the castle, you are not to even look at her, do you hear me? You are not to mention her to anyone or spread the word about her supposed willingness."

"Supposed!" Owen scoffed. "With all due respect, my lord, she was the one who knelt at Eric's feet, and you should have seen the way she rode our—"

"I care not what she did or how. You are not to even *think* about her ever again, in any manner whatsoever."

He gritted his teeth because he knew exactly how she behaved with men. She had told him and he had seen it for himself. That day she'd ridden him like a woman on the edge of sanity, with a desperation verging on panic. There had been a distant look in her eyes, as if she had not really been there, but in another place, separate from her body ... It was her way to remain sane, he now understood. As to her kneeling at men's feet, it was no proof of willingness, it was just another protection strategy. She'd explained why she preferred not to be taken. Attack was the best form of defense. As a skilled swordsman, Matthew knew all about striking before your opponent had a chance to hurt you.

"She didn't want to be taken, by you or anyone," he told the men, wondering how much to reveal of Branwen's past. It was not his decision to make. But he could impress on the men the importance of never behaving in such a way again, with her or any other woman. "She didn't want to be hurt, so she thought it preferable to give you what you wanted before you took it by force."

"By force!" At least the men appeared suitably horrified at the notion. "My lord, we would never have—"

"No, I know." At least he hoped so. The men Connor employed could not be such bastards. He trusted his brother to seek out reliable, honorable men to work for him, even if they did not always behave toward the womenfolk with finesse. "But from now on make sure you stay well clear from her, or any woman who does not give you her explicit agreement to be bedded, or you will have to answer to me for your actions. Am I clear?"

"Perfectly clear."

There was nothing more to say. He stormed out of the barbican in search of the master of the hounds. Next, he had a pup to find.

∽

"Will you be Gwenllian's godmother?"

Branwen swallowed, looking at her friend. Could she accept? Only a few weeks ago she would have recoiled at the thought of being so close to a child, but oddly, admitting out loud to Matthew why she was wary of being in contact with babies had made it easier to bear being with the little girl. Or perhaps the fact that Gwenllian had been born in her house had created a bond between them. Whatever it was, for the first time she was considering accepting the request. She looked at the baby, asleep in her mother's arms and her heart melted. Yes, perhaps she could agree to become her godmother.

Still, she was an odd choice, there was no denying it.

"Why me? You must have dozens more prestigious—"

"There is no one better," her friend interrupted. "Elena has already agreed, but I need a second godmother, and there is no one I would want in your stead. She was born in your house, and you and I have been friends since we could talk together. 'Tis only fitting. I wanted you to be Siân's godmother, but Gruffydd objected, and convinced Gwyn we should choose someone he deemed more suitable. I am ashamed to say I did not fight the decision."

Esyllt's eyes, usually so full of warmth, became hard as ice, as they did every time the man was mentioned.

The Welsh lord, who'd been a friend of her late husband, had revealed his true, manipulative nature when he had forced her into a marriage with an Englishman, with the sole aim of disposing of him. Fortunately, he had happened to choose for her a man she loved and who loved her back, and he had failed in his attempt to kill him. He was still being pursued by Connor, who meant to make him pay for what he had made himself and his wife go through. Unfortunately, the wildness of the Welsh landscape made it all too possible for someone who wanted to vanish to do just that. It might be years before he was caught, if he ever was. Unfortunately, he might never be made to suffer for his villainy.

Just like Bryn, whose status protected him from retribution.

Who would take the side of poor women against a powerful lord?

"I'm sorry. I know what you went through because of Gruffydd," Branwen murmured, pushing the unpleasant thought out of her mind.

"And I know what you went through with that vile man, what you are still going through." Her friend's voice wavered. "You made me swear not to tell Connor about it. I honored your wishes, but it's eating at me. Please say you have changed your mind and want the man brought to justice. He needs to be punished."

"No. I can't."

A tense silence filled the room, then eased. The two friends had never been able to stay angry at one another for long.

"Say you will be Gwenllian's godmother." Esyllt placed a kiss on her daughter's forehead as she pleaded. The gesture was so full of love that Branwen's heart leapt. She knew then that she would accept.

"I would be honored. Who is the godfather?" she asked even though she had already guessed the answer. There was only one man Connor would want to stand as godfather to his first child with his beloved new wife.

His beloved, trustworthy brother.

Esyllt gave her a slanted look, confirming her suspicions. "Who do you think? I swear I'm not out to trick you. It's only, as I said, that you are the most obvious choice and Matthew is as well. He never got to be Connor's first children's godfather because his late wife had numerous brothers and insisted on choosing one for each of their three girls. But we now have no one to please, and you've both been by our sides through it all and we love you dearly."

Branwen fell into her friend's arms, the baby's warmth nestled between them.

"I love you too. And I thank you. I will be Gwenllian's godmother."

They remained locked in the embrace a moment. Then Esyllt gave her a watery smile. "Let us go tell Connor then. He will be very pleased."

They found him by the east tower, deep in discussion with a group of guards. When they approached, his squire led the men away and only Matthew remained. Branwen could barely meet his eye. They hadn't seen each other since the morning they had woken in the same bed. Fortunately, Connor's pleasure at seeing his wife and child prevented the moment from being awkward.

"How is my girl today?" he asked, holding out his arms to the baby as eagerly as if he had not set eyes on her for weeks.

"She's well," Esyllt answered, handing him the little girl. "And she is soon to have the perfect godmother."

Branwen blushed when Connor dazzled her with a smile. "Thank you for accepting. I know it means a lot to Esyllt."

"It means a lot to me too." It was a first step toward a new life, one where she could allow herself some joy.

She could not help stealing a glance at Matthew, who was part of this life. His eyes were warm with approval. Had he guessed what it meant to her to have agreed to let a child into her heart? Probably. He was a very perceptive man, and he now knew her story. They remained with their eyes locked a long moment, while the new parents decided on the best way to dress their daughter for her impending christening.

Heat started to invade Branwen. Men had looked at her in lust more times than she cared to remember, but never with such admiration. It was disconcerting, but it made her feel special, worthy. It was just like it had been the other day, when he'd asked her forgiveness for doubting her motives. Despite her past, he seemed honored to be her friend. Although ... they weren't friends exactly. So what were they?

More to the point, what could they be?

The baby started to fuss, providing a welcome distraction.

"Give me Gwenllian back," Esyllt said with a sigh. "I guess she will be hungry again. After all, she's only fed three times this morning."

Her husband gave a throaty laugh and leaned in toward her. "I understand all too well her desire to be at your breast night and day, my love. Would that I could do the same. Only I wouldn't stop at the suckling."

Though he had spoken in a low voice, Branwen heard the heated declaration. She suspected her cheeks had gone the same crimson color as Esyllt's, and Matthew's smile only confirmed it. He'd heard his brother's words as well, and he was enjoying her reaction.

Connor straightened up and cleared his throat, as if suddenly aware he was not alone with his wife.

"Why don't you go sit in the sun over there? It's a nice day, and God knows these are rare enough. You should make the most of it."

"Yes, you're right."

Branwen followed her friend to the bench by the chapel and watched as she started to nurse her child as naturally as if she had been a simple villager. It was in moments like these that she understood how the two of them could be friends despite their difference in rank. Esyllt had never thought herself more important than anyone or above any task required of her. This had been remarkable enough when she'd been the local lord's daughter. Now that she was Lady Sheridan, it was all the more astounding.

Even as he talked with Connor, Matthew watched the two women huddled together in the sunshine, one as fair as a spring day, one as mysterious as a dark night. He could only guess what Branwen would be thinking while her future goddaughter fed. Would she one day get her own babe to nurse thus? He certainly hoped so, for he didn't doubt she would make the most loving, the most protective mother. Hadn't she proved it time and time again? With Eirwen? With Elena?

"Lord Sheridan?"

Matthew started. Lost to his contemplation of the women, he hadn't seen that a short, thin man wearing a cassock had stopped in front of them. The man was obviously wondering which of them was the lord of the manor. Connor straightened up, used to having strangers hesitate between the two of them.

"Good afternoon, Father. I'm Lord Sheridan. How can I be of service?"

"I'm Father Paul, the new priest in town. I thought it was time I introduced myself to the local lords who haven't come to me yet. I've been in post for a month already."

Matthew gave the man an assessing glance. Though he appeared to be quite young, his hair had already started to recede along his temples. That and the fact that he seemed imbued of his self-importance gave the effect of a man twice his age. He'd not lost time in suggesting that Connor should have been the one going to him, rather than the other way around. There was also an obsequious air about him, as if trying to ingratiate himself in noblemen's good graces had become as natural as breathing to him. The way Connor had stiffened seemed to suggest he shared this assessment. His brother had never liked people who pandered to him just because he was noble, and ignored others around them. The man had not even looked in Matthew's direction once, evidently thinking him of no importance compared to the lord of the manor.

"I was sent here by the king himself," he continued, oblivious to their reaction. "He thought it expedient to ensure his subjects stationed here to protect his domains had access to a clergyman speaking their language and sharing their feelings at having been sent to a hostile land, and I can only agree with him. It didn't take me long to see that the Welsh are every bit as uncivilized as they are portrayed."

Unsurprisingly, this speech did little to endear himself to Connor, who was married and deeply in love with one of those supposed barbarians. Matthew, who had admittedly at first thought the land inhospitable and the people somewhat rough, was astounded to hear the man express such an uncompromising opinion in front of strangers.

"I see. If such is your opinion, I can imagine you are eager to meet my neighbors. What with them being lords and ladies in their own right, you should find them to be more refined than the villagers you've seen since your arrival. Or is it all Welsh people you despise?"

Matthew worked hard at containing his smile. Connor was mocking the priest, but the man missed the sarcasm.

"I'm afraid I cannot imagine how their rank will make any difference. The men are a violent lot and the women shamelessly debauched." As he spoke, he nodded to the bench where Esyllt was restoring order to her dress while Branwen held little Gwenllian tenderly against her chest.

Matthew's blood boiled. Admittedly, Esyllt's shoulder was bare at the moment but only the worst kind of bigot could have ascribed a lewd intention to the scene. She'd been feeding her child, for Christ's sake, not exposing herself to the men around! His dislike for the man crystallised into something like hatred, and there was no prize in guessing what Connor would be thinking.

He rounded on the priest, all pretense at politeness or sarcasm abandoned.

"That is my wife, Esyllt, you're talking about," he warned. "I do hope you're not suggesting she is a promiscuous wanton for doing nothing more than feed our daughter—in other words, doing the most natural and beautiful thing in the world. I might as well tell you that I will not take too kindly to anyone casting aspersions on her character."

The ice in his voice matched the frost in his eyes. For all his pleasant manners, his brother had a temper on him, and nothing was guaranteed to rouse it faster than slurs against his wife. Had Father Paul been a knight rather than a priest, he might well this moment be pinned to the wall with a sword at his throat.

"No, my lord, of course not," the priest hastily assured him. "It was not my intention to speak ill of Lady Sheridan, as you can imagine. I meant the other one, the one next to her, the villager with the black hair. You wouldn't know of course, but I'm afraid she is not suitable company for your lady wife. You see, I know for a fact she—"

"Branwen is my wife's dearest friend. I will not have anyone call her unsuitable."

"You might if you knew what depravity she is—"

"The matter is closed." This was Connor at his most commanding and there was nothing Father Paul could do. "Matthew, please escort the good priest back to the gate. I'm afraid I have no time to see him now. I was on my way to see Father Rhisiart to make arrangements regarding Gwenllian's christening."

The blow had the desired effect on the priest. "The christening! You're not seriously considering having a Welsh—"

"No. I'm not considering it. It's already been decided. My daughter is half Welsh, her godmother, Branwen, and my beloved wife are Welsh, we live here at Castell Esgyrn. Gwenllian will be christened by our Welsh priest. Father Rhisiart is a good man, not prone to spreading slander, which is more than I can say about others."

With those words he walked over to the bench where the two women were watching him with quizzical looks. Even from where they were, they would have picked up on the tense atmosphere. Matthew could not blame them. He was bristling with rage and it undoubtedly showed.

Doing his best to behave normally while still in full view of them, he led the priest back to the barbican, as he'd been instructed.

As soon as they had passed the gate, he grabbed him by the collar, barely resisting the urge to slam him against the wall. Father Paul's shock at such treatment was obvious, and even justified, but Matthew was past caring. He would not have anyone call Branwen a debauched, shameless barbarian in his presence and leave unchallenged.

"Listen to me, priest," he growled in his ear. "There are only two ways you could know about Branwen's supposed depravity." Either he had heard in confession one or more of the Englishmen who had bedded her, or he had approached her himself, in search of forbidden pleasures. Clergymen breaking their vow of chastity was not unheard of, and Father Paul had struck him as a weasel from the start. He wouldn't put it past him to try and abuse his power in that manner, especially with people he thought so lowly of. "The first one makes you a gullible bigot, the second one a lecherous bastard. One will earn you my contempt, the other, my fist down your throat. Which is it?"

"I-I don't know what you're talking a—"

"How do you know about Branwen?" he cut in, not in the least interested in his protests. "You only arrived a month ago, and yet you seem awfully familiar with her alleged wantonness. So what have you done to her?" The mere idea of this man forcing himself on Branwen was enough to make his skin crawl.

"Done to her? Nothing, I swear! Me, have carnal knowledge

of a creature of Eve?" The man shuddered. "I would never sully myself thus."

His outrage was not feigned. He was truly repulsed at the notion of lying with a "creature of Eve," whatever that was.

Matthew released him. If the priest had not gone to Branwen himself, that meant he had heard about her from the English soldiers stationed in town. The despicable men would have gone to him to be absolved of their sins, no doubt so that they could go find another woman and start all over again. His stomach roiled at such hypocrisy. Who were the depraved ones in that story? Certainly not Branwen.

"You heard about her during confession then. What lurid tales did your parishioners regale you with?" Considering what he knew, he could imagine all too well. The whole thing was sickening.

"I cannot tell you what I heard. I'm bound to secrecy, as you must know. The confession is sacred."

Yes, so sacred that the pompous fool had used the knowledge he'd gained that way to warn Connor about Branwen's unsuitability.

"But how many of your precious countrymen told you the truth, I wonder? How many admitted to you that they had in fact raped her?" he hissed. "Let me guess, they didn't. They merely said they needed forgiveness for having been lured into sin by a Welsh temptress."

"They stood no chance, that much is certain." Now that Matthew was not holding him any longer, some of the priest's inflated confidence had returned. "The woman is a Jezebel, capable of every act you can—"

"She is as much a Jezebel as you are a saint," Matthew spat. "And I am telling you she never wanted any part in it. Unlike you, *I* know her, you see."

"No need to ask how."

Was the man determined to get hurt? Matthew glared at him and took a step back, not sure he would resist the temptation to hit him if they carried on this conversation. But he would not create problems for Connor, who had managed to keep his own temper on a leash.

"Go, before I show you it is not the Welsh you should worry about, but me."

Chapter Eight

The following day, Branwen came back to Castell Esgyrn to attend Gwenllian's christening. She entered the chapel in a dreamy state, wondering how she was going to survive being at the center of attention. To add to her discomfort, Esyllt was not there. No matter how much she had pleaded to be allowed to come, Father Rhisiart had been inflexible. New mothers were not supposed to attend their own child's christening. She would be going to the banquet afterward, but she simply could not enter the chapel until she'd been churched in a few weeks' time.

It was already quite a break with tradition to have waited for so long to have the little girl baptized, the priest would not condone another irregularity.

It had surprised Branwen that Connor had chosen a Welsh priest who barely spoke English to christen his daughter, instead of Father Paul, the English priest newly arrived in town but, in truth, she was relieved. The man had a way of looking at her that made her ill at ease. Worse, she had the uncomfortable notion that the argument in the bailey the other day had been caused by her.

All in all, it was better she did not have to see him today.

Soon, she found herself standing by the font, between a radiant Elena and a splendidly dressed Matthew. In his dark tunic embroidered with silver, over which his blond hair gleamed like gold shavings, he was the exact counterpoint to his dark-haired brother, who was dressed in white with highlights of copper. Connor was magnificent, every inch the powerful lord, but she only had eyes for one man. It was just like it had been at the lake. She could not see anyone else when Matthew Hunter was in front of her, whether dressed or half naked.

As for her, she had never felt better.

Esyllt had given her one of her most beautiful dresses, arguing that she might never be able to fit in it again, now that she had borne her daughter. It was a gown of pale green velvet, with tight sleeves adorned with exquisite embroidery representing holly leaves and bright berries. Her friend had smiled when Branwen had commented on the choice of decoration. Ladies usually went for less prickly motifs.

"Connor once told me I reminded him of holly, which gave me the idea to decorate his favorite dress with it."

Holly, really? Branwen couldn't help but arch a brow in surprise. Couldn't Connor have come up with a more flattering compliment? "That's ... romantic," she said uncertainly.

"It is." The way Esyllt's eyes sparkled told her there was more to this story than she was letting on, a secret between husband and wife. Maybe odd as it was, the compliment had hit a chord. "I will have to embroider another dress with holly leaves now. Or perhaps a shift. I think he would like that."

There had been such an expression on her friend's face that Branwen had blushed all the way to her toes. That shift would no doubt end up ripped to pieces when Connor tore it off his willing wife's body.

After that she had not been able to refuse the gift and was

now glad of it. Amongst noble people dressed in all their finery, she would have felt at a disadvantage in her usual clothes, like the only gray peahen amidst resplendent peacocks. In the beautiful dress, she was able to relax, confident in the fact that she didn't stand out in any way, on the surface at least.

Of course, deep down, she was nothing like them.

Father Rhisiart started to pour water onto little Gwenllian's forehead, and Branwen had to force herself to look. As important as the moment was, she could barely concentrate. Having Matthew next to her was creating havoc within her. Did it show? Did she appear as flustered as she felt? She hoped not. It would not do to betray her inner turmoil while all eyes were on the group standing by the font.

Dear Lord, Matthew mused, as he tried his best to focus on what the priest was saying, Branwen was transformed today. Or rather, revealed.

He'd always known she was a true beauty, so he was not surprised to find her so alluring, but the cut of the dress she'd been given emphasized her slender curves, the shimmering velvet drew the eye to her flawless skin, and the color made her eyes glow like pure gold. There was also a becoming flush to her cheeks, which he liked to see above anything else. Too often he had seen her pale as a corpse. But today, all the ghosts from her past seemed to have receded to the back of her mind, allowing her true self to shine through. The result was staggering.

She truly was the most perfect woman he had ever seen.

The ceremony passed in a blur. He did all that was required of him, held the baby when she was handed to him, repeated all the necessary words at the right moment, but his mind was not on the task at hand, with Branwen so close to him, calling out to every part of his body. His eyes were irresistibly drawn to her, his arms wanted to wrap around her waist, his fingers itched to stroke her skin, his lips ached to taste her mouth.

And his groin ... His groin had never been tighter.

Later, during the banquet, it was even worse. As she'd been placed next to him, he did not resist the temptation of pressing his thigh against hers, even though he fully expected her to recoil. To his delight, she did not, and he spent the whole evening with a hard shaft pulsing in rhythm with his heart. Even the sugared almonds brought at the end of the meal could not distract him from the sweet-smelling woman by his side.

Forget the exotic delicacies, he wanted to eat *her*.

The banquet finally came to an end, and the dancing began.

"I wish I could dance, but alas, my body will need a little bit more time to recover before I can attempt it," Esyllt said with a sigh when the musicians struck up a lively tune. Not wanting to dance while his wife was incapacitated, Connor had gone to speak to the local lords and the two of them were the only ones left on the dais. "Are you not going to join in the revelry, Matthew?"

"I don't think so." Not with his body throbbing the way it was. His tunic was too short to hide the effect Branwen's proximity had had on him. Though she had left his side a moment ago, he was still hard, had been hard all day, or so it seemed. "You know I rarely dance." Thankfully that was true, so his refusal might not raise any comment.

"I know, but if ever an occasion warranted it, this is it."

She didn't seem offended, but he felt guilty all the same because she was right. He should be dancing, joining in the celebrations. "Let us strike a bargain, my lady. If I one day get my own children christened, I will dance."

As he said the words, his gaze flicked over to Branwen, who was deep in conversation with one of the ladies standing by the lavishly decorated door. She wasn't dancing either, he noticed. Perhaps after all she endured week after week, she couldn't bear the idea of being held by a stranger. It would not surprise him, and in truth, he was relieved. He wasn't sure how he would have handled seeing her in another man's arms. At the least improper gesture on his part, he would have pounced, and he had no wish to create a scene at his niece's christening.

"I will hold you to that promise," Esyllt said with a smile, "and hope to be there to see it."

"You will, as you will be chosen to be godmother." He gave a gracious tilt of the head, but at the moment, the possibility of having children seemed remote. If Connor had really put an end to his matchmaking efforts on his behalf, then he could not see himself getting married anytime soon.

Esyllt let out a tinkling laugh. "Come, Matthew. Everyone will understand you choosing Connor as godfather, but your future wife might prefer to choose a friend of hers to act as godmother."

"Yes. Well. That still doesn't rule you out, does it?"

"No. I guess it doesn't."

For a moment he couldn't understand why his sister-in-law's eyes were twinkling.

Then he thought back to what he had just said. Somehow he must have imagined Branwen holding his firstborn child. Had he not pictured her as his wife, he would not have assumed Esyllt would be chosen as godmother. It was clear from the way Esyllt was looking at him that she had reached the same conclusion.

What was happening? Only the other day he had thought that he would be proud to have a child with Branwen, no matter what her past. And then he had failed to be relieved when she had assured him she could not have fallen with child from their encounter. Now he was planning their child's christening.

He cleared his throat and excused himself. The state of his body notwithstanding, he could not remain here, at the risk of getting more confused than he already was.

Alone in bed at last, he had no choice but to bring about the release that had been boiling in his spine whole day long. The image of Branwen in her green dress as she'd stood by the font with Gwenllian in her arms seemed branded on the inside of his eyelids, and provided all the excitation he needed. A few strokes were enough to take him over the edge, and he bit his lip so hard to stop himself from shouting Branwen's name when he finally erupted that he tasted blood. What the devil had that been about? Never had he pictured a fully dressed woman when giving himself pleasure, much less one standing in a church, much less one with a babe in her arms.

Ashamed, more bewildered than ever, he fell flat on his stomach and tried to go to sleep.

Branwen was the first person he saw in the great hall the following morning. It was still very early, which might account for the fact that she was alone. The lords and ladies who had stayed at the castle overnight were used to keeping different hours. But of course she was no lady, merely a hardworking villager.

"Good morning, Branwen."

"Good morning, Matthew."

She flushed when he sat down next to her and he was reminded of all the things he had imagined doing to her the night before, while he'd pleasured himself. If he had been able to flush, he would be flushing himself right now. What she would think if she knew what he fantasized about doing to her didn't bear thinking about. The last thing he wanted was for her to think him as depraved and selfish as the men who took their pleasure with her.

Except he knew he was anything but depraved, and as to being selfish ... The thing he wanted to do the most was give her pleasure, show her what her body was capable of. He didn't want to *take*, he wanted to *give*. His whole life, spent controlling his own urges, learning to please his lovers instead of bedding them, ensured he had the skill to make her feel the beauty of her woman's nature.

She deserved to be caressed, licked, devoured, soothed, and then sent back to heaven.

He cleared his throat and helped himself to a slice of ham. This wouldn't do. At this rate he would soon go mad.

But how could he stop himself from dreaming about holding her when she looked so beautiful? When she was the first, the only woman he had ever possessed? When he knew she had never known pleasure and thought herself unworthy of it? When he could make her see how glorious it could be between a man and a woman?

It took a passing comment from one of the servants to make him realize she was not wearing the velvet gown anymore, but her usual woolen dress. He had not noticed the change, because she appealed to him as much today as she had the day before, dressed in a lady's finery.

And that's when he understood.

Branwen's transformation, which he had attributed to the green gown that hugged her curves the day before, had nothing to do with the clothes she'd worn, and all to do with *him*, and what he now thought of her.

Their heartfelt conversation the other day, and the way he had sprung to her aid, that was what made her eyes sparkle, her skin glow, her stance more relaxed. She was at ease with him, because he now knew the truth about her and he had not judged her. She was gratified that he had confided in something he had not told anyone else, namely that he'd been a virgin before what had happened between them. There was this new connection between them, a bond stronger, somehow more significant than the joining of their bodies. They had bared their souls and doubts to one another. When they had made love, both had been fully dressed, and they had not even made eye contact.

Now they had seen each other for who they truly were.

"How have you been?" he asked, feeling completely at a loss.

They hadn't had time to talk in private the day before, and it had suited him well, as he felt strangely intimidated in front of her. This new awareness of one another was daunting, much more than physical intimacy.

"I'm well, thank you."

Was it his imagination, or was she just as intimidated as he was? It sounded like it.

"I'm famished," he said, a pitiful attempt at normal conversation. But it was true. Too on edge to behave normally the night before, he had not eaten much at the banquet. "What about you? Would you like something else to eat?"

"I'm all right."

Despite her answer, he could not resist placing another slice of venison pie in front of her, because now that he thought of it, he wasn't sure she had eaten much last night either. Here was the chance to ensure she at least ate her fill today. She thanked him with a smile but did not touch the pie.

"I know you paid Daffydd with your own money the other day," she said instead, sounding slightly breathless.

"Daffydd?" Matthew frowned. He wasn't familiar with the name.

Branwen lowered her gaze, as if regretting bringing the subject up. "The owner of my cottage."

Of course, the one he had paid to leave her alone and repair the roof of her cottage. Matthew ran a hand around the back of his neck, feeling caught out. How had he not guessed that she would go to Connor to thank him for ensuring she wouldn't have to pay her rent for a year, and that his brother would betray the fact that he had no idea what she was talking about? His real role in the whole affair had been revealed.

"I'm sorry I lied," he said, "Only I thought you would not—"

"It's all right, I understand why you did what you did. Sometimes people do bad things for noble reasons. And I thank you for insisting." She lifted the venison pie to her lips and bit into it, as if to say he had done the same thing just now, offering her food when she had said she didn't need any. Once she had swallowed her mouthful, she looked at him again. "And he came to repair the roof just as I was leaving to come here, so you don't need to come to check that he honored his promise."

Matthew nodded. He was relieved her roof would finally be repaired, but he was not sure he liked the idea of having no excuse to go and see her at the cottage.

"Are you leaving now, then?" he asked, helping himself to a handful of nuts. The rest of the ham he'd just cut himself lay uneaten on the trencher. His appetite seemed to have suddenly deserted him.

"Yes."

In truth, Branwen would have liked to remain a bit longer at Castell Esgyrn, but there was no reason for her to stay, even if she was loath to go back to her cottage. Solitude was getting harder and harder to bear.

"Before you go, I have something to give you." Matthew's eyes were sparkling with something akin to mischief, and for a moment he put her in mind of a little boy. It was an odd thought because he definitely was all man. "Stay here. Don't go anywhere before I come back. Please," he added after standing up, as if worried his request had sounded like an order. It hadn't.

While he was gone, Branwen took another bite of pie and tried to bring her heartbeat back to a normal rhythm. There was something different about Matthew that morning. Or was it her? Them?

She didn't know, and she wasn't sure how to handle it.

When he reappeared a while later, he was followed by a grey wolfhound. Stopping in front of her, he nodded toward the animal who reached almost to his thigh, despite being obviously still a puppy.

"This is Silver. But of course, you could choose a different name for him."

"Why would I do that? Silver suits him, with this streak of white hair over his nose." She ruffled the dog's shaggy head. He was adorable, with big, soulful eyes that looked straight into hers.

"Because he's yours now."

Branwen froze, her hand between the pup's ears. When she stared at Matthew in amazement, she saw that the brown in his eyes had become almost black.

"M-mine?" she stammered. "You're giving me a puppy?"

"A puppy who will soon grow into an impressive dog." He rubbed the back of his neck, no longer mischievous boy or confident knight. "I'm thinking he might come in useful to deter men who come knocking at your door at dawn, demanding their rent or ... at any other time of the day for any other reason."

He was giving her protection and company, the two things she needed the most. Overwhelmed by emotion, Branwen fell to her knees and hid her face in the dog's fur, giving him the hug she wished she could give Matthew. A mere moment ago she'd been thinking she didn't like the idea of returning home alone. Now, thanks to Matthew, she wouldn't. Giving her this dog was the most thoughtful thing anyone had ever done for her.

"I don't know how to thank you." She was already in love with the pup. "I know I should refuse but I—"

"You should most definitely do no such thing. Please, take him with you." He hesitated. "It would put my mind at ease to know you're not alone."

Branwen nodded, unable to do otherwise. This could be the answer to all her prayers. With an intimidating dog by her side, ready to jump at their throat at the least hint of menace, men might think twice about accosting her. Could Silver be the savior she'd needed all this time? No, not Silver. He was a dog—he would only be doing what he'd been taught to do without knowing why his new mistress needed protecting.

The real savior was Matthew, who knew about her situation and wanted to put an end to it.

"Thank you." The two words barely passed her lips.

"Think nothing of it."

The expression on his face was indecipherable. Either he didn't want to betray his own emotion or he thought he had done nothing extraordinary. It was possible, but she knew it was not the case. The dog might not be enough to offer her the safe life she dreamed of, but that Matthew cared about her, and wanted to help, meant the world to her.

He gave Silver a pat on the head, then looked at her.

"Come, Raven. If you think you've eaten enough, I will get you back home."

∽

"I will ride to Sheridan Manor on the morrow," Matthew announced, as he and Connor broke their fasts together the following morning. Having insisted on nursing her baby herself instead of taking a wet nurse, as was customary for ladies of rank, Esyllt was still in bed, catching up on her sleep. "The news of little Gwenllian's birth will need to be announced there."

His brother arched a brow. "I daresay. But I can send one of the men to do that. You don't have to go in person."

Oh, but he did. Not for the reasons he'd invoked, but

because he needed time away from the Welsh temptress who had managed to turn his life and his mind inside out. If he took his time, he could easily be away from Esgyrn Castle—and her—for a month. More might appear suspicious, but a month was feasible.

With luck, by the time he returned, he would be cured of his infatuation with Branwen. Because he could not let it overtake his life in the way it was threatening to do, in the way it had already started to do, or he would go mad.

He was falling hard for a woman who had every reason to hate men, and Englishmen in particular. It could lead nowhere save heartbreak. Matthew was discovering to his horror that he had a heart to break after all. Because it had always cost him little to keep women at bay, or at least to remain detached with the ones he allowed near him physically, he'd thought himself immune to the feelings other men experienced.

How wrong he'd been to think himself safe—how naïve!

He had not met the right woman, that was all.

The night before, he had brought himself to climax not just once, but twice, remembering the way Branwen's sweet body had rubbed against his as they'd ridden to the village on Midnight's back. It had reminded him of the way she had ground against him and welcomed him inside her body that day in the solar, how she had squeezed him tight to precipitate his pleasure. It had been blinding, unlike anything he could have imagined.

What he wouldn't give to relive that moment. Not just because of the pleasure he had experienced in her arms, but so that he could do everything differently.

It had taken all his inner strength not to stop the horse and beg her to let him take her there on the forest floor, but he had managed not to do it. The humiliation of a refusal, he could have dealt with. His pride had sustained worse blows. But the look of horror and fear in her eyes, when she thought him no better than the other men who thought her a whore at their disposal, he could not have borne. And so he had kept his mouth shut and done his utmost to keep the throbbing in his groin under control. It had worked, but he was not certain he could do it a second time.

His mind was made up.

He needed distance and time to adjust to the new developments in his life.

"If you're sure ..." Connor started, looking at him oddly. Damnation, his brother had guessed there was more to his desire to be away from Esgyrn Castle than the wish to announce the birth of his niece in their childhood home. He'd always been perceptive that way, and Matthew wouldn't be surprised if Connor had seen that something had changed in him.

Yes, it was high time he left.

"I am. Please be so kind as to write your instructions for me sometime today," he told him curtly. "I leave at dawn."

∽

The white raven was back.

Branwen stared pensively at the animal perched on the highest branch of the beech. How odd that such a rare bird should decide to live near her cottage when she was named after him. It was as if he knew they shared a connection. She remembered how Matthew had once teased her about her name's meaning and smiled, before closing her eyes.

Matthew. Would everything remind her of him?

As if to answer that question, at that precise moment Silver put his head on her lap and whined, demanding a caress. Yes. It seemed that everything would remind her of her savior, first and foremost the dog he had procured for her. Less than two weeks after his arrival at the cottage, the pup had already fulfilled his mission. The day before, an Englishman from town had approached her as she was gathering wood in the clearing, and drawn her into his arms, intent on tumbling her to the ground. He'd reeked of drink and been more forceful than her usual attackers, and she had feared an assault that would leave her hurting for days.

But before she'd had time to utter more than a cry of alarm, the faithful animal, who'd taken to his new mistress as quickly as she had taken to him, had leapt on him and scratched his back so severely that the man had fled in fear for his life, blood dripping down his body.

For a long time, Branwen had remained in the clearing, hugging the panting pup, crying in relief and gratitude combined.

"Thank you for being here for me," she told him, ruffling his silvery fur. "I hope you don't miss your old master as much as I miss him."

The dog gave her such a penetrative stare that she took him into her arms.

They remained there a long time, locked in an embrace.

"What's the matter, Branwen *bach*?" Her mother's voice suddenly cut through her thoughts. Lost to her musings about Matthew, Branwen had not heard her approach. "I worry about you. I've never seen you like this."

It was not surprising, for she had never been like this. But since Matthew had burst into her life, she had not been herself. Kissing him, pushing him on the chair to ride him like she would ride an impetuous stallion, and getting frightened by the intensity of the sensations it had provoked within her, sensations she had never felt before and was afraid of, confiding her greatest shame first to her friend and then to him, becoming a godmother ... It had been a bewildering, intense few weeks.

But now he was gone and she felt bereft.

Two days after the christening, she had gone back to Castell Esgyrn to see Esyllt and Gwenllian, hoping to spend a moment with Matthew while she was there, only to hear he had gone to England and no one knew when he would be back. The news had been a blow. He'd left, without even telling her.

After they had kissed, she had wished he would disappear. Well, it seemed she had gotten her wish, just when she was starting to wonder how she would ever bear to have him out of her sight.

When would he be back? And what if he decided to stay in England? Why would he not? It was his home. The mere idea that she would never see him again had her guts twisting in dread.

"It's about a man, is it not?" Carys asked. Branwen could only nod. It was about a man, but not just any man. It was about one of the only men who had treated her decently, the one person who had given her the means of changing her life and some hope for a better future. "The man who was here the other day, the one with the kind eyes?"

Kind eyes. Yes, that was one way of describing him. Kind eyes. Endearing smile. Mouthwatering body. Generous spirit. Not only had he not judged her after hearing her story, but he'd been on her side, unquestionably, and made her feel worthy of respect. His reaction had made it possible for her to regain some of her dignity back. After the encounter with the drunk Englishman, and with Silver by her side, ready to pounce if need be, she felt strong enough to make her refusal plain to the next man who came to her demanding access to her body.

Finally, she could see a way out of this nightmare.

If ever anyone had been given a priceless gift, this was it.

"Yes. It's about him."

"He's nothing like the others, I don't think." Carys said

softly, cocking her head. "I could tell straight away, from the way you looked at him—and he at you."

Branwen crumpled from the inside. Her mother knew about the other men? Lord, she had hoped it wouldn't be the case. But the relief of not having to hide her pain from her was overwhelming. She fell into the woman's arms, sobbing.

"Oh, Mam, he's nothing like them at all."

And she wanted him back.

Chapter Nine

"You'll never guess what happened on my last day at Sheridan Manor."

Matthew paused, knowing the news he had to impart would be a shock to Connor, even if, admittedly, less so than it had been for him. But it would have consequences, consequences he was not sure he was ready to face. Regardless, he could not take the cowardly way out and stay silent. This was too important. All the way from England he had mused on the extraordinary turn of events and pondered on what to do next, without managing to find a satisfactory answer to that question.

With luck, talking about it with Connor would help.

He emptied his cup of ale and sighed, because as serious as it was, the whole affair had not been enough to chase all thoughts of Branwen from his mind. He missed her. A month away from her had failed to achieve what he had hoped it would achieve. Quite the contrary. Though nothing obliged him to go back to Wales, he had been on his horse at dawn on the day he'd assigned for his return. It even crossed his mind, as he thundered through the gate of Sheridan Manor and set off on the west road, that he had only decided on a date to avoid rushing back to Esgyrn Castle as soon as he'd arrived and delivered his message to the people of Sheridan Manor. Yes, all in all, this trip had been a waste of time.

Except that it had yielded an unexpected result.

He afforded a small, mirthless laugh. It seemed that even with hundreds of miles between them, Branwen could have a positive effect on his life. Was it a sign? Was someone trying to tell him something?

"A man came," he finally said, "asking to see my mother."

"Your mother?" Connor arched a brow. "But she died more than twenty years ago."

"I know. The man clearly had no idea what had happened to her, though, and he was devastated to hear of her death because he …" His voice trailed as the tragedy of the situation hit him anew.

"He what?"

"He'd been hoping to be able to finally marry her."

Thunder striking at that moment would not have stunned Connor more. Matthew knew the feeling. It had been the same for him.

"*Marry* her? What the hell?"

"I know. It's the last thing I ever expected to be told, and if I'm being honest, I don't quite know what to make of it."

Matthew sighed and ran a hand through his hair. That was the least he could say. He and Connor had always imagined his father to be a nobleman visiting the manor, seducing, or more probably, raping the young maid called Rose, and then leaving without worrying about the consequences of his actions. He had always hated thinking that he was the product of an assault on his mother, the son of such a dishonorable, selfish, irresponsible man.

And now, aged thirty, he was finding out that, far from raping and then abandoning her, his father had only done what he thought right by another woman. He was not a nobleman who had taken advantage of his status at all, but a humble carpenter who had been sincerely in love with a woman he had met as a young man. He had not washed his hands of them, but instead had tried to face his responsibilities

It was good news, undoubtedly, but it still required some time to adapt. His whole life had been built on a lie. All the pain, the humiliation, the anger he'd gone through, had been for nothing. He had no reason to hate his father. Rather he should feel sorry for him. And he did.

Dear God, what a mess.

He popped a sugared almond into his mouth before carrying on.

"Once he'd recovered from the shock of learning that the woman he was looking for was dead, he explained it all to me. He met my mother as a young man of barely twenty when he came to a fair in town. He had come to meet a fellow carpenter his father had told him about, and she had gone to help her aunt sell her wool. Between them, the attraction was immediate and they started seeing one another that very night. When he left a week later, they had fallen in love."

If one was to believe the man's story, and there was no reason not to, it had been that simple. The cruel irony of it was not lost on Matthew. After years wondering, or rather worrying, about what had happened between his parents, he was told they had just been two people in love.

"My mother had been working at Sheridan Manor for a couple of years then, and was loath to give up your parents' employ. As you can guess, not many noblemen treat their servants so well. So they agreed he would go back home and settle his affairs. Then he would find a place in the village next to the manor and they would get married."

"Just like that?" Connor was incredulous, which was little

wonder. Matthew, too, had been incredulous at first. This was such a far cry from the story he had imagined all his life that it was difficult to accept. Who fell in love at first sight and decided to get married within the week, anyway?

A niggling feeling prickled at the back of his neck, because something was telling him it might not be so difficult to believe after all. With the right person, it could well happen like that.

"Yes, just like that," he muttered. Connor nodded, as if he'd himself come to the conclusion that it was all too possible. "And they would have honored their promise, I believe. But when he returned home, he found out that a farmer's daughter he'd been bedding the previous summer was carrying his child. Devastated, he came back to tell my mother that he had no other choice but to marry the woman and give the child the name and protection it deserved."

Matthew's throat tightened when he remembered the look of agony in the man's eyes as he'd told him about it. Thirty years later, he clearly still felt the heart-wrenching pain he'd felt at the time, when he'd had to abandon the love of his life to face his responsibilities.

"Your mother agreed to that?" Connor said slowly. "God forgive me, but I wouldn't blame her if she had not."

"Me neither. But yes, she did. She agreed that he had to do the right thing by the woman, and she renounced her claim on him. She argued that she had fallen in love with a good man and she didn't want him to turn into a dishonorable scoundrel, even for her. And so he went back to his village with a heavy heart and married the farmer's daughter." Matthew paused again. What a sacrifice that must have been. "His wife died last month, and so he came back to Sheridan Manor, hoping my mother still worked there, or that someone would know where he could find her, because he meant to finally honor his betrothal to her, made all those years ago."

Without a word, Connor poured two cups of mead they emptied in unison, eyes locked. There was a wealth of understanding in the green eyes so different to his own brown ones.

"The news of her death must have been quite a blow."

"That is putting it mildly."

"But there's something I don't understand. If he was so bent on marrying one woman to protect the child she was carrying, he would have been devastated when he found out Rose was also with child. Your mother would have been justified in demanding he looked after you both and he would likely have agreed. Marrying her would have been impossible, but at least they could have—"

"She never told him about the babe. About me," Matthew whispered. He'd thought the same thing. They could have drawn some happiness from the fact that they had a child together. "I know because the man told me they had never seen one another again after he'd told her about the farmer's daughter. It was the only way. He didn't wish to be unfaithful to his wife, and he knew he would not be able to resist temptation if he ever saw the woman he had never stopped loving."

"Dear God. What a tragedy."

Matthew nodded. "It seems we were wrong all along. My parents loved each other, they were good people who were denied the chance of living their love." What a waste that had been. And how different would his life have turned out to be if his parents had done what they wanted to do and married.

After a long moment, Connor planted himself in front of him. "Tell me ... tell me you told the poor man about the babe. About you."

Matthew stared back at his brother, or rather at the man who had never really been his brother. This might be the last time he got to call him by that name. Now that they knew where he came from, Connor might well send him back to his real family.

"I did not tell him. I could not," he murmured, not brave enough to look him in the eye. "After so many years hating the man who had sired me for taking advantage of my mother and abandoning her to face the shame of my birth alone, I could not bear to see that he was actually a good, honorable man who'd never stopped loving her and wanted to give her the life they had wanted together. He renounced what he wanted so he could offer his son a chance at a respectable life. I could not tell him it had all been in vain, because he'd left another boy to grow as a bastard."

He bunched his fists. That half-brother he did not know had had all Matthew should have had. A name, a family, parents who raised him together.

"Matthew, it is not your place to—"

"I could not do it, Con," he repeated. "The man was devastated when I told him the woman he'd hoped to be reunited with had been dead for more than twenty years. I didn't see what good it would do to tell him that he'd not only denied them both happiness, but that he'd done the very thing he'd wanted to avoid. The whole reason he'd broken his and my mother's hearts was to ensure a little boy didn't grow up as a bastard. How do you think he would have felt to know he had left me behind?"

"I understand, I do," Connor said. "It would not have been easy. But he has the right to know he has another son. And knowing he has you might even go some way into easing the pain of losing your mother."

Matthew started. How had he not thought of that? At least the poor man would know there was something left of the love he and Rose had shared, that someone would remember it. Yes, it might give him some comfort.

"I promise to think about it." He braced himself for the next sentence, the one that would cost him the most. "I will leave now."

"Leave? Why? You've only just arrived."

The weight on Matthew's chest became unbearable. He was not announcing his intention of going on a pointless errand, but of leaving forever. But to go where? That was the question. He didn't have a place here anymore, but he wasn't sure of the welcome he'd get in his father's village or even if he wanted to go. He didn't want to leave here, leave *her*.

Branwen.

Amidst his trouble, it was all he could think about. If he went back to England, any chance of ever building something with her would be ruined and he wasn't sure he was ready to accept that, as much as he had wanted to take his distance from her.

He shook his head to chase the disturbing thoughts away. Things were complicated enough as it was.

"We always assumed I was the son of a nobleman, even if of questionable character. Now we know I'm nothing of the sort. Your parents were generous enough to raise me as if I were half-noble, but the bastard son of a maid and a poor carpenter cannot keep posing as Lord Sheridan's brother. I will therefore—"

"You will do nothing save get these silly notions out of your head," Connor snarled, coming to within an inch of his chest. "You are the only brother I've ever had, and we didn't raise you as such because of an elusive connection to a nobleman, but because you and I got on from the moment we started sparring, and you've always been there for me. You are not going anywhere."

"But I—"

"No *but*. You are not going anywhere and that's final." He grabbed him by the shoulders, the fingers digging into his flesh as if to force the meaning of his words to penetrate deep. "I will not allow it. God on the cross, why would you do that to me? Can you imagine me having to tell Jane and Siân they are never to see their beloved Uncle Matthew again? And Esyllt? I wouldn't know any peace until I had dragged you back here kicking and screaming. So there will be no more talk of leaving. Are we clear? Forget everyone else, *I* could not bear it. And if all that is not enough to convince you, remember that you once saved my life, and might do it still. I just can't afford to let you out of my sight. I don't want to."

By now a lump had formed in Matthew's throat. He'd not dared hope Connor would react that way and he was overwhelmed. "We are clear. Thank you. It means a lot to me."

"No problem, *Brother*." The emphasis on the last word caused him to close his eyes. "It means a lot to me, too, to have a man like you by my side."

The two men fell in each other's arms. Matthew thought he might well start crying if the embrace lingered a moment longer. Fortunately for his dignity, it didn't.

"Oh. And a letter came from the king while I was in Sheridan Manor," he informed Connor when they finally drew away. It was best to revert to business as usual. "He wanted you to bring your Welsh bride to court so he could meet her and see the success of his plan for himself."

"I ..." His brother made a grimace, as he had anticipated. "I'm not sure I—"

"It's all right. I already answered, saying that the birth of little Gwenllian had left Esyllt too weak to travel. The midwife advised her to rest, and there is no telling how long she would need to remain bedridden, unfortunately."

There was a pause, during which Connor absorbed what had been said. Matthew knew he wouldn't object to him answering in his stead, as he usually handled all his correspondence, but he might object to the manner in which he'd done it.

This was the king they were talking about, not just an unimportant local lord.

"You lied to the king?"

"What else could I do to justify a refusal and protect you from retaliation at the same time?" Matthew shrugged apologetically. "It's all too plausible that Esyllt should be incapacitated, and no one will tell him any different, will they? The next time he asks, he will be told she is too heavy with child to undertake the journey, the time after that, that she is sadly attending her sick mother, or fell from her horse and is still abed recovering. I haven't decided which yet. He will soon get tired of asking, don't worry. He will never set eyes on her as long as I'm here to read the letters."

"Yet another reason for you to stay." Connor looked at him a long moment. "Tell me. How did you know I dreaded Edward seeing Esyllt?"

"Why do you think? He is a famous lecher, and your wife is far too lovely to be put under his nose. I thought you'd want her well away from him."

"I do. But I'm amazed that you of all people should understand how a husband would feel about these things."

Connor had a point. Only a few months ago Matthew would not have thought anything of the king's request. Indeed, he would probably have encouraged his brother to comply, in the hope of furthering his prospects. But now ... now everything was different. The idea of putting a beautiful woman in contact with a man who would only consider her fair game was unbearable. The king would not heed Esyllt, or indeed Connor's protests, if the need to have her took him, and that could only end in disaster.

Why did he feel so strongly about it? Perhaps it was due to Branwen's story. Perhaps he feared the consequences of such a meeting for Connor, because his brother would hardly stand aside and let anyone, be he the king of England, rape his wife. He would end up being tried and executed for treason when he cut him to shreds.

Whatever the reason, he was not going to risk his sister-in-law meeting the king.

"Well, in any case, worry not. As long as I'm here, Esyllt is safe."

If only the same could be said of Branwen.

∼

"Guess what I heard. Lord Sheridan is in the village right now. He's come to inspect the progress of the work being done on the new mill. On his own."

Something about the way the man said those last three words caused the hairs at the back of Branwen's neck to rise on end. That morning she had gone to the market in the nearest village for a change. Since Matthew had left, she'd been at a loose end, like someone waiting for her life to resume its normal course after an unwelcome interruption. An excursion to the next village was as good a distraction as any. She was now glad she had come because her interest had been piqued when she'd overheard the three men standing by the vegetable stall. As she was rummaging through the cabbages in the hope of finding an acceptable one, they had started to talk about Connor. They sounded so full of bile that she had shuffled closer, suspecting she might catch something that would be useful to her friend's husband.

It did not take her long to see that she was right.

The men were not just complaining about their new English lord, they were plotting to get rid of him.

"Here is our chance," one of them said with a sinister grin.

"He won't know what hit him. We'll strike as he heads back to the castle he stole from us."

"Aye. And I know the perfect place for it," his friend added in a whisper. "Let us leave now, so as not to miss him. Such an opportunity might not present itself soon, or ever again. We'll go get Rhodri and Siasper on the way."

With those words, the men headed toward the woods she could see in the distance.

The place of ambush.

Branwen forced herself not to move until they had disappeared from view, so as not to raise their suspicion. She could not let them know they had been overheard by someone sympathetic to their enemy, but she had to go and warn Connor that men were ready to ambush him on the way back to Castell Esgyrn.

Abandoning the cabbage she'd finally found, she rushed to the mill.

The men could not be allowed to put their vile plan to execution. Not only did no one deserve to be killed in such a way, but Connor was married to her friend, and father to her children. Esyllt's life would be destroyed if anything happened to him. And that was not all. English though he may be, he was a fair, efficient lord and careful administrator who took good care of his tenants.

For the sake of everyone, he needed to live. She could not have his death on her conscience, not when she had the means to prevent it.

At the pace she was walking, it did not take her long to reach the mill. As she approached, she let out a sigh of relief. The villagers had been misinformed. The man standing by his horse, ready to mount, could not be Connor. He was too broad, too blond, too—

Relief was instantly replaced by intense joy, the likes of

which she rarely felt when he turned enough for her to see his face in profile.

"Matthew!" she exclaimed, running up to him. He was back. For too long she had dreaded being told he had decided to stay in England.

"Branwen, what are you doing here?" His hand instantly went to the hilt of his sword and he scanned the horizon. Evidently he'd assumed someone was in hot pursuit of her, and that was the reason she was running to him. "Is everything all right?"

"Yes. Or rather, no." For a moment, lost to her joy, she had forgotten all about the threat on Connor. "I came to see Lord Sheridan. I was told he would be the one to inspect the mill?" She craned her neck to look behind Matthew. Was he around? Or had he already left? Fear spiked through her. Was she too late after all?

"He was supposed to come, but he couldn't make it. Gwenllian kept him up these past two nights, and he and Esyllt are barely able to stand." Branwen knew that, as well as being a loving husband, Connor was an excellent father, involved in the caring and raising of his three daughters. It therefore didn't surprise her to hear he had been the one soothing his baby at night, rather than send for a maid, as many nobles were wont to. "He sent me to tell the carpenters he would come next week."

Relief swept through her. If that was the case, he was safe, and the men would be waiting in the forest for naught. A week gave her plenty of time to warn Connor not to go anywhere unescorted in the future.

"Are you going back to Castell Esgyrn now?" she asked Matthew.

He glanced at the horse whose reins he was still holding. "Yes. I was about to leave."

"Could you take me there? That way I could help with little

Gwenllian, or at least allow the poor parents some respite. I am her godmother, after all."

Matthew gave her a strange look. "I'm sure they'd be grateful for the help, but you would do that, when being with children is painful for you?"

She reddened, touched that he would be concerned for her. He hadn't changed while he'd been away, he was still as solicitous as ever. "It's painful, but it's also a great pleasure, and if I am never to have any children of my own, then I might as well make the most of others."

"That's very brave of you." He sounded so proud of her that she felt warm all over.

"I'm not sure that can be called bravery."

For a moment he looked as if he wanted to comment, then he nodded. "Come then, I'll take you to the castle."

Without further ado, he hoisted her up the mighty stallion's back, then climbed on behind her. The heat of his body against her caused Branwen's eyelids to flutter in delight. He was really back. She could start living again.

"Here. Are you comfortable? Fortunately, Raven is just like Midnight, strong enough to carry us both."

"You named your horse Raven?" she asked, turning to look at him over her shoulder. She'd heard from Esyllt that Connor had bought a pair of matching grays the other week, but she hadn't known one of them would be for Matthew. She should have guessed. "But ... he's white as snow!"

"He is, isn't he?" The smile he gave her reduced her insides to gruel, and she had to face forward again for fear of betraying the fact by the color blooming on her cheeks. "But I thought you of all people would not object to the choice of name. White ravens do exist, you know, though I would have bet my life on the contrary only a few weeks ago. I saw one outside your cottage, in fact."

"I know the one you mean. How odd that he should choose to live here."

"Yes. It's almost as if nature had taken it upon itself to teach me a lesson." There was laughter in his voice. "It seems that Welsh people know what they're doing after all, and your parents made a good choice when they decided to name you after such a creature, as rare and beautiful as you are."

My, the man did nothing by half. Matthew's compliments were as wonderful as his insults had been painful.

"What did Connor name his horse?" she asked, instead of commenting in any way.

He gave a chuckle that once again put her in mind of the little boy he had once been. "He called him Snowball, if you'll believe it. It's so ... uninspiring, don't you think?"

"Yes. Though I suspect Jane and Siân had a hand in the choosing of the name, for whoever heard of a knight giving such a name to his destrier?"

This time he barked a rich, masculine laugh. Her insides rippled. "You're most probably right, I never thought of that. It will be the girls' doing and he was unable to refuse them, the fool. Well, fortunately, they didn't help me choose Raven's name."

Branwen was confused. Was he saying that he had named his horse after her? He had to—only someone who knew what her name meant would have thought of a name like Raven for a white animal. So what did that mean?

"Shall we?" she asked. They still hadn't moved an inch. What was Matthew waiting for?

They set off at a brisk walk, and it didn't take her long to see that she would have to lean back against Matthew's chest if she wanted to be comfortable. They had sat on the same horse when he had taken her home after Gwenllian's christening, but she didn't remember being so affected by their proximity then.

Usually when she was in a man's arms it was to give him pleasure. It was nice to be able to enjoy the moment without worrying. It was more than nice, it was a revelation, because she trusted this man absolutely. There was nothing to fear from him, she could relax, safe in the knowledge he wouldn't make her do anything she didn't want to do.

She could make the most of the wonderful warmth and scent of him.

"You didn't bring Silver with you?" Matthew asked after a while.

"No. Unfortunately, the poor beast hurt his paw yesterday, walking on a thorn. I left him with Mam and Eirwen when I decided to go to the next village. He will be well looked after. They dote on him, as do I." She swallowed. "I cannot thank you enough for the gift of him."

She heard a growl and felt a rumble against her back. "You mean, that you had cause to be grateful he was with you while I was away?" Matthew's voice had never sounded more dangerous.

Should she tell him about the encounter with the Englishman in the clearing? He sounded aggrieved enough already. But she could not lie to him, not after all he had done for her. Besides, it might ease his mind to see that his plan had worked. He had given her the dog in the hope that the animal would provide her with the protection she needed, he would be relieved to see it was the case.

"Only once."

"That's once too many."

Yes. But it had also been the first time in more than ten years she'd been able to escape a man's assault. It gave her hope for the future. "It's a start. My reputation as a willing woman, if we can call it that, started slowly. Why should the reverse not be true? Bit by bit word will spread that anyone who tries to approach me will be torn to shreds. This, combined with my new determination to make my opinion known, will eventually ensure I am free of hassle."

"Yes. By the time you're ninety, men might have stopped assuming you'll welcome them with open arms," Matthew grumbled. "Forgive me, but I don't think you should have to wait another day, never mind another decade to live the life you deserve."

"No. Me neither."

But there was no other choice.

For a moment they traveled in silence, Branwen relishing the feel of Matthew's arms around her. As soon as they entered the forest, however, she could not help but tense up. Were the men still here, hidden in readiness, or had they heard that Connor had not come after all and abandoned their ambush?

"Are you uncomfortable with our proximity?" Matthew asked, picking up on her sudden stiffness. "Forgive me, I should have thought. Would you rather I—"

"No. I will never be uncomfortable with you," she assured him. Not after what they had shared, physically and emotionally. She knew he was not about to pounce on her, or hurt her in anyway. "But you see, the reason I came to the mill was to—"

It happened in the blink of an eye.

Three men jumped in front of Raven, causing him to rear up in fright. Only Matthew's skill and strength prevented them both from toppling off the horse's back. When he finally brought the stallion under control, two more men came from behind, blocking their retreat.

Not a man to be so easily daunted, even when outnumbered five to one, Matthew drew his sword, then ordered his mount to attack. The beast, trained as a warhorse for just such a precise purpose, felled one of the men with a neat kick to the head. Another assailant was cut when Matthew swung his arm in a great arc. But in spite of his bravery, he was soon pulled down from his horse and brought to his knees.

"You English bastard! You're going to wish you'd stayed where you belong."

"Castell Esgyrn and the land around it is ours! Your king had no right to give it to you."

It took Branwen a moment to realize they were convinced they had captured Connor, as planned. But of course, why would they think any different?

"Wait! This is not Lord Sheridan!" she told the men, doing her best not to fall from the stallion who was fighting the hold one of the attackers had on his reins. In vain. The man, for all his villainy, knew how to handle horses, even nervous ones. "You're making a mistake, he's not who you think he is."

Matthew didn't speak more than a few words of Welsh, and understood very little, so it was up to her to speak in his name. Why had she not explained to him why she had come to the mill! He might have guessed what this was about then, and somehow tried to prove his identity. As it was, he had no idea why the men had ambushed them. He clearly thought them intent on hurting *her*. She could see the way he kept glancing at her that he was worried about the men's intentions regarding her.

But for once she was not the target.

"Yes, this is Lord Sheridan," the tallest of the men answered. "I don't know what tales he's told you to get between your legs, but he is. I was there last year when he and his retinue of accursed Englishmen arrived. It's him, there's no doubting it. I served at the banquet that night and I saw him sitting on the dais next to that traitor, Esyllt ferch Llewelyn."

Dear God, this was worse than she had supposed. The men not only hated Connor and wanted him dead, but because against all odds, Esyllt had found happiness in the marriage she had been forced into, they considered her a traitor. Branwen's chest tightened in dread. What fate did they have in store for her friend?

She brought her mind back to the present, because there would be time enough to warn the people at Castell Esgyrn of the villagers' ill will. For now, she had a more pressing problem on her hands. Unfortunately, if one of them had been present at Esyllt's welcoming banquet to the English a year ago, there would be no convincing the men Matthew was not Lord Sheridan. She knew all about how the two brothers had swapped places that night and how Matthew, not Connor, had been introduced as the groom. The tall man was right. Matthew had spent the evening on the dais next to Esyllt, while Connor had sat with the rest of the guests in the hall.

The mistake had been rectified amongst the people at the castle since then, of course, but the villagers might not have heard about the misunderstanding in the first place, or that it had been sorted out. In any case, even if they had, the fact remained. Matthew was English, and therefore a target in the men's mind. Who he really was, was of no import in the end, only his nationality.

"Get down, wench, we are going to give him what he deserves."

Branwen steeled herself. Matthew was still on his knees, surrounded by four irate men, and he had no idea what was going on. It would be down to her to save him. Unfortunately, she could not fight her countrymen off, but there might be a way to stop them all the same. Pretend to agree with them and force them to "kill" Matthew in a manner that guaranteed his survival.

It was a risky option, but the only one available to her.

She jumped down from the saddle and threw him a glance she hoped conveyed all she could not say. He was to trust her, even if it appeared as if she was turning against him. It was the only thing she could do. She could not warn him, as she could not be sure the men didn't understand English. More and more Welsh people made sure to at least have a knowledge of the invaders' language, and she needed them to believe she was on their side for the trick to work. Though she would gladly have seen her countrymen flogged for what they were doing, she had to act the part of the patriot Welsh woman.

Matthew's survival depended on her.

"You cannot kill him outright," she told the men, eyeing up the weapons in their hands. The tallest one was carrying an axe, and the others were armed with pitchforks. Though not conventional, the weapons were deadly enough. Matthew would be skewered before he had time to blink if one of them gave the signal to strike.

"Why not? It's no more than he deserves." The man who'd spoken bared his yellowed teeth in a grimace. Branwen repressed a shudder. She couldn't betray any disgust toward them, not until Matthew was safe.

"Because if you do, his death will be avenged by his English friends and more innocent Welsh people will suffer as a consequence. You need to make it look as if it were an accident." She looked at the lake down below meaningfully. By a stroke of luck, they were not far from a ledge that overlooked it, and an idea had popped into her head. "I happen to know he doesn't know how to swim, because when you stopped us, he was telling me he'd always been afraid of water, ever since he almost drowned as a child. Perhaps he could really drown as a grown man, and see how he likes it."

The notion of Matthew being afraid of anything, much less water when she had seen him swim like a fish, was ridiculous. But the more ridiculous she made him appear, the better. In her experience, prejudiced fools were quick to believe the worst of their victims. It was their weakness. You could rely on them being condescending.

And the men seemed to take the bait. The one who had come from behind Raven, and been cut by Matthew's sword, nodded.

"The wench is right. A drowning would serve just as well and would guarantee no one comes after us in retribution."

The tall one grunted. "I suppose she has a point. I have no desire to die for doing what's right."

Hope surged within Branwen. Perhaps this mad plan would work. She pointed at the pitchforks, pressing her advantage. "If they found him with more holes in his body than a sieve, questions will be asked, and the culprits will be searched, and found. You will never get away with it, and escape retribution. Do you wish to be hanged, or worse, for doing what every Welshman would do in your place?" She purposefully used the word *man*, to distance herself from such villainy. There was only so far she was prepared to go. "You don't want to have to go in hiding after today, and live the life of an outcast. Think of your families."

This was supposing they had families they cared about, of course, and people who loved them in turn. One could not be certain with weasels only brave enough to attack a man five to one. But to her relief, two of them nodded and looked at the others, as if to persuade them.

"My wife's just had a babe," Yellow Teeth declared. This time Branwen couldn't help but to shudder at the thought of the poor woman enduring his attentions. It wasn't hard to guess he would be no gentle lover. "Our sixth. I cannot place them in such a situation for an English maggot whose life is not worth a rat's fart. It will be as the girl says, an accidental fall into the lake, followed by a drowning. What say you?"

"Aye. A fall and a drowning."

With those words, the four men took hold of Matthew and lifted him up, two by the arms, two by the legs.

Branwen stiffened. A fall? She hadn't mentioned a fall. What did the men intend to do? She took a step forward but no one was paying her any attention. Holding Matthew as they would a sack of flour, they were heading toward the edge of the cliff. Understanding dawned. They were about to drop him into the water from where they were.

That hadn't been the plan at all.

"Wait! You can't—"

Too late. Under her horrified gaze, they threw Matthew over the ledge.

Chapter Ten

How long before he hit the water down below, Matthew wondered, as his arms flayed hopelessly in the air. How big was the drop? Did he have time to try and twist his body so that he didn't land on his back? He had to, as he would die otherwise. Forget the drowning, he would not even have time to understand he was underwater before he lost consciousness. He saw it all with painful clarity. The way his body would shatter with the force of the impact, the graceful collapse of his corpse as it drifted slowly down to the bottom of the lake.

With a grunt, he bunched his stomach and straightened his legs. Ensuring he hit the water feet first would be the last thing he did. He could not let the men win. It was not even about him. The image of Branwen's wide eyes when she had understood they were about to throw him over the ledge was stamped into his brain. This could not be the last time they'd ever seen each other. He let out a howl.

A heartbeat later he hit the water surface—feet first.

There was no time to congratulate himself, no point in dwelling on the excruciating pain shooting up his legs, he had to get out of the icy water. Now, before it was too late, before he either drowned because he needed to breathe or his limbs seized up from cold. Using his arms to propel himself, since his legs didn't seem to be able to do anything but cause him pain, he pushed himself up, or at least in the direction he hoped was up. For a dreadful moment he feared he was going the wrong way, burrowing deeper into the murky waters instead of swimming toward the light. His lungs were burning, it wouldn't be too long before he simply had to take a breath. Whether it would be air or water remained to be seen.

Finally, he broke through the surface, and he inhaled the cool spring air. Was it his imagination or could he actually smell the sap running through the trees, the flowers swaying in the fields yonder? Never had anything smelled sweeter.

Panting, he looked around to get his bearing.

He was not too far from the shore, he was relieved to see. It would not take a swimmer as good as he was long to reach it. The only problem was, he could barely use his legs, which felt as if thousands of pins had been stuck in them. Well, no matter, he just had to make it—there was no other choice. One thing pushed him on. It was not survival, it was thoughts of Branwen on her own in the middle of four men bristling with unspent violence. He was pretty sure the one his stallion had kicked was out of action, but the remaining four might want to compensate for their inability to hack him to death by making the most of her warm body.

If that was the case, if they touched one hair on her head, he would find them, and he would kill them slowly, painfully. And to be able to do that, he needed to be alive. He needed to swim.

So he swam. It was the only way.

Kicking, groaning, spluttering, he pushed on. Later, he could rest; later, he could worry about the pain radiating through his body. For now, he had to get out of the water. At long last, he landed on the gravel beach, cold and stiffer than a piece of wood.

Turning onto his back, he closed his eyes and focused on breathing a moment.

He'd made it.

Now all he had to do was find Branwen.

Where was Matthew? Branwen was getting frantic. Even going straight down through the bushes, it had taken her forever to reach the shore of the lake. More than once her feet had slipped on loose pebbles, causing her to land on her buttocks and slide down the steep slope in a ridiculous, never mind painful manner. Once, she had even gone tumbling head over heels, scaring herself half to death before being stopped in her tracks by a more substantial bush. It would have been good news if the bush in question had not been bristling with prickly leaves that had torn at the skin on her face and arms.

It had been folly to jump straight down into what was essentially a ravine, of course, but she had wanted to reach the lake as quickly as possible, so as to assist Matthew when—*if* by some miracle—he emerged from the lake. Add to that the fact that she would not have stayed alone with the four ruffians for all the gold in the world. They wouldn't be above jumping on her to alleviate the frustration of not being able to kill an Englishman, expectant wives notwithstanding. She of all people knew that when a man's blood was raised, not many things stood in his way. Fortunately, they had not run after her, preferring not to risk their necks for a tumble they could get with any village wench.

It had been reckless on her part, but Branwen was not afraid. She just wanted to reach Matthew and see that he was safe, because rather than save him, she might well have caused his death.

When she finally reached the lake, there was no one to be

seen. Her heart started to hammer in her chest. Why wasn't he here? Because he'd already left, not thinking for a moment that the woman who had caused him to be flung over the precipice would bother to come after him, or because he'd been stunned by the fall and was now dead, lying at the bottom of the lake?

Pressing a hand to her forehead, she scanned the horizon. Nothing. Where *was* he? For a moment she thought she might faint or retch. Then a movement to her left caught her eye.

Matthew.

He was dripping wet, his blond hair almost as dark as hers because of it. His clothes were molded to his body, allowing her to see each of the bulging muscles she remembered from the day she had seen him emerge from the lake naked. He appeared unsteady on his feet, but at least he was standing. Relief washed through her. He was alive—he hadn't drowned.

As she watched him approach, a flicker of unease mingled with her relief. Even from where she was, she could see that his jaw was set, and his eyes were sending sparks. Was he angry at her? Of course. If he had not understood her plan and thought she really wanted him dead, he had every reason to be. But it didn't matter. He could be angry all he wanted, as long as he was alive.

Before she knew what she was doing, she ran to him and threw herself in his arms. "Oh! Lord, you made it, you made it!"

His arms closed around her, not the suffocating hold of an enemy intent on punishing her for her betrayal, but the protective embrace of a man who cared for her. He was not angry, not at her at least. Everything within her relaxed.

This could have ended up disastrously wrong, but he was here, warm in her arms.

"Branwen." The word was little more than a whisper. The hold around her tightened. "Tell me the men didn't ... they didn't touch you? Or harm you in any way?"

She shook her head, relishing the feel of him against her. He was standing, talking, and he didn't even appear injured. It was a miracle. For a long moment she stayed in his embrace, then she drew back. It was time she explained what had happened and why.

"They weren't here for me, but to kill you. They thought you were Lord Sheridan."

He gave a wry smile. "Yes, that much I had understood. I imagine it was because they had seen me at Esgyrn Castle when I impersonated him last year."

"Yes, that and the fact that they'd heard he'd come here today to inspect the mill. That was why they were waiting in ambush, why I tensed up when we entered the forest. It was not because I didn't want you to touch me, never that," she explained hurriedly, her body starting to tremble with the aftermath of all that had happened. "I should have told you from the moment we set off that I'd overheard the men at the market and what their plan was. I'm sorry, I cannot think why I didn't, it was stupid of me, because if you'd known, we could have gone another way, or tried to—"

He placed a finger on her cheek, interrupting her mad rambling. Then he pulled her into his arms again. "Don't worry about it. There's no harm done in the end."

No, perhaps not, but there could have been.

"I'm sorry," she cried out, drawing away from him, not ready to be comforted yet, when she still needed to gain absolution for what she had done. "I know I was the one suggesting the men let you drown, but I had to do something to give you a chance at survival, I could not let them pierce you with their pitchforks or kill you outright. But I never imagined they would throw you off the cliff!"

"You did well, and I understood what you were trying to do the moment you opened your mouth," he soothed. "That was remarkably quick thinking on your part. You saved my life, Raven. You gave me a chance to save myself, and I seized it. I thank you."

Clutching at his tunic, she started sobbing. Yes, it *had* worked, she *had* saved his life. He was safe, he was whole, he was holding her. She now just had to accept it was all over.

He tightened his hold around her and she let out a cry. Her arm. In her relief at seeing him, she had forgotten all about it. She had felt a bolt of pain shooting up her elbow when she had gone tumbling head over heels earlier but had ignored it. She didn't think anything was broken, but something clearly wasn't right either.

"You said the men hadn't touched you!" Matthew cried out, holding her at arms' length to examine her. "But you're hurt."

"They didn't touch me, I swear. Only, I hurt myself by climbing down the cliff after you. I think I twisted something when I fell."

He looked at the cliff behind her and recoiled in horror. "Don't tell me you went down that slope?"

A smile teased her lips at his reaction. "It was the quickest way to get to the lake."

She would not admit to Matthew that she had also been afraid of staying alone with the men. He already seemed on the brink of explosion. Instead, she bared her forearm and saw that her elbow was swollen, and had taken on a reddish hue.

"Oh, Branwen, did you have to rush so?" Matthew remonstrated, his touch as gentle as his voice was rough.

"Of course, I did. I had to see for myself that you hadn't been killed by the fall."

Muttering to himself, something about stubborn Welsh women, Matthew struggled out of his wet tunic. With the sodden material, he fashioned a kind of sling, explaining he wanted to hold her arm bent tight against her middle. "Not moving it will stop the worst of the pain."

"But you will freeze to death without your clothes," Branwen protested meekly. An arched brow indicated the ludicrousness of the statement. Indeed, in the wet tunic, he would not be any warmer than he was now, simply dressed in his undershirt.

"Hold still, stop arguing and let me do what needs to be done," he scolded. "I'm hoping the cold of the material will help numb the pain somewhat."

It might, she acknowledged. And having her arm held securely was a relief, as he'd said.

Once the sling was securely in place, he placed a brief kiss on her lips. She was too stunned to react, not that she would have protested. It had been a sweet, tender proof of his concern. She tried to swallow past the lump in her throat. "Thank you."

"No. Thank *you*. You're the one who saved my life. No one else in the entire world can make that claim," Matthew said, before adding pensively. "Do you know, I think I understand now what Connor feels when he thanks me for rescuing him from that bastard Gruffydd. I always thought his reaction was exaggerated. We both know I have done nothing he wouldn't do for me. But it is odd to owe your life to someone, and knowing you cannot express your gratitude adequately or repay the debt."

"Yes."

Branwen had a good inkling of what that might feel like. Matthew had not saved her life, per se, but he had given her a more bearable one and hope for a different, better future. It was as he'd said ... she would never be able to express her gratitude or repay the debt for what he'd done.

He gave a slanted smile, as if he'd guessed all she was not saying. Then he placed another swift kiss on her mouth. Her throat went dry. Matthew Hunter's kisses, whether passionate or gentle, were like nothing else.

"Let us go. If we walk fast, we might be able to reach the castle before nightfall."

At that, Branwen started sobbing again. Dear God, but she was an emotional mess right now.

"I'm sorry, but the men took Raven," she said, wiping at her eyes. "Before I jumped down the cliff, I heard them say they would get a good price for him. I should perhaps have stayed and tried to stop them, but I think there was nothing I could have done to—"

"No. You were right not to confront them. We'll get Raven back, don't worry. It will not be so easy for villagers to sell a destrier without raising suspicion or attracting attention." The look in his eyes hardened. "The important thing is that they didn't hurt you."

"They didn't."

"Good. I couldn't have lived with myself if anything had happened to you."

That was something they had in common then, because she couldn't have lived with herself either if anything had happened to him.

He took her free hand in his and placed a kiss on it, every inch the dashing knight in front of his lady. "Come. It's time to go."

∽

"Dear me, what happened to you two?"

Branwen knew she would look a fright with her scratched face and her arm wrapped in the sling and, of course, Matthew was in his shirt and wet braies. No doubt they both looked exhausted as well. Her friend would understandably worry.

"I'll tell you everything. But first I need to sit down."

"Of course." Esyllt led her to the fur-covered bench, her eyes full of concern. "You'll also need something to drink, I daresay."

"Thank you, some ale and bread would be most welcome," Matthew said, coming forward. The bedraggled clothes notwithstanding, he didn't appear any the worse for his ordeal. Branwen shook her head. Apparently, the man was made of iron.

"Bread! I think we can do better than that."

Servants were called, and soon a lavish feast was spread on the trestle table by the window. Branwen forced herself to eat her rabbit pie slowly, as she related the attack to her friend. She kept the more disturbing details out, like the fact that the men wanted Connor dead and her punished for being happy in her marriage to an Englishman. She would reveal them later, when the shock of today's ordeal had worn off.

By the time they had eaten and drunk their fill, it was pitch dark outside, and Branwen could feel her eyes closing of their own accord.

"Thank you, Esyllt. Now I will need to speak to Connor," Matthew said, dipping his fingers into a bowl of scented water. "Branwen can come with me if she's not too tired."

"Of course." She was tired, but not so much that she could allow any delay in informing Connor of the situation.

Esyllt led them straight to the solar, where they found him writing a letter. He took one look at them and dropped his quill into the inkpot.

"Who?" he asked Matthew, fury blazing in his green eyes.

"Villagers. The attack was aimed at you, though."

"Dead?"

"Not all of them."

Branwen was stunned by the bluntness of the exchange, but

evidently the brothers did not tiptoe around one another, and why should they? Connor needed to be told the danger he was in.

This time, she let Matthew relate the story of how they'd been set upon. She noticed he was leaving out unnecessary details for now, much as she had done.

"You need to find those men, Connor!" Esyllt exclaimed, once he had finished. "They need to be punished."

"I will find them, never fear, but you, dear wife, look about to collapse. What I need right now is to get you into bed. Come, love, there's naught that can be accomplished tonight save making sure you get the rest you need."

With those words, he swept Esyllt into his arms, the gesture so loving it brought a lump to Branwen's throat. How good it must feel to be loved and looked after thus. But of course she would never know the joy of having a loving husband taking her to bed because she was tired from looking after his newborn child.

The door closed on the couple and silence fell in the solar. Alone with Matthew, Branwen started to shake uncontrollably.

"I think ... possibly the skeletons Castell Esgyrn was named after belonged to two hapless souls who'd been thrown into the lake and drowned," she said, her voice barely above a whisper. "They ended up in a ditch all alone, forgotten by everyone."

A sob escaped her lips at the terrible notion. It could have been Matthew's fate today. He could have died, and his body left to rot in a forsaken place.

"Hush, sweet. I didn't drown. It's over." Without waiting for permission, he engulfed her into his arms, careful of not putting any pressure over her injured arm. "It's over. You saved me, remember? It's over."

She nodded against his chest. Yes, she had saved him. But how would she ever forget the horror piercing her gut when she had seen him plummet to his possible death? The memory would haunt her for years to come.

"You need to change your clothes," she mumbled. Even after a whole afternoon of walking, they were still damp. How had she not thought of this before? He needed warming up as soon as possible. It would not do for him to have survived the downing in the lake only to die of a chest cold.

"And *you* need a good night's sleep. You look about to collapse."

With those words, he swept her into his arms, much in the same way Connor had done for Esyllt a moment earlier.

Too stunned to protest, too grateful to resist, too tired to do anything, she allowed her head to rest against his chest and let herself be carried to a room where a brazier was burning. By the time he'd deposited her onto the bed, covered her with the blanket and given her cheek a gentle stroke, she was already half asleep. The events of the day had taken their toll.

"How is your arm?" Matthew asked solicitously, unwrapping the tunic that was holding it in place.

"Better. I can hardly feel the pain anymore." She had been right to think the injury was not severe.

"Good. I'll leave you to sleep then. Tomorrow you should feel your normal self."

He made to get up but Branwen stopped him with a hand on his leg. "No. Stay here with me, please." Her words were slurred, but even with her brain addled by fatigue, she knew she wanted this. She had almost lost him today, she needed the reassurance of knowing he would be fine, she needed to feel him, warm and solid, next to her. They had already slept in the same bed once. What harm could it do to do it another time? None. "You need to warm up. With us two in the bed, you'll do that a lot faster."

She had expected to have to argue, promise it was really

what she wanted, but to her surprise and relief, he immediately agreed. Perhaps he'd secretly hoped to stay with her and hadn't dared ask for permission. It mattered not why, as long as he did.

"Very well. I'll get undressed now," he said in a deep voice. "I'll remove everything this time, I'm afraid. I cannot lie in bed in my wet clothes and I have no other with me. Just close your eyes and go to sleep, I'll join you in a moment."

Without further ado, Matthew started tugging at his clothes, not embarrassed in the least to have a witness. Branwen fought to stay awake. She wanted to watch, and see his naked body gilded by the low-burning flames in the brazier, but her eyelids were too heavy and the bed too soft for her to resist the lure of sleep. She caught a glimpse of a smooth, broad back and rippling shoulders, the curve of a spine.

A moment later, she was asleep.

Chapter Eleven

The creaking of the door was not loud but still enough to stir Branwen out of her slumber. She turned her face to the door, where the glow of a candle was painting the stone wall gold. Before she could wonder who the mysterious visitor might be, a head popped in through the crack.

"Branwen, are you all right?"

Esyllt.

"Yes, I'm all right," Branwen breathed. She was more than all right, nestled in the warm, comfortable bed she had been allocated. "What are you doing here at this time?" Through the narrow window, she could see the black, star-filled sky. It was the middle of the night.

"I've just finished feeding Gwenllian, and now I'm wide awake so I thought I would check on you. Can I come in a moment?"

Branwen hesitated. Something was lurking at the back of her mind, something that seemed to suggest it would be better if her friend stayed where she was, but she couldn't think what it was.

"Yes," she finally said, still not finding the will to move. She was wrapped in the most wonderfully warm cocoon, and the room looked cold.

Esyllt stepped forward, the light she was carrying illuminating the bed.

Three things happened at the same time.

Esyllt's mouth fell open, the cocoon of blankets moved, and Branwen remembered what it was that had bothered her.

Matthew was in the bed with her. Naked, and wrapped around her like a vine.

He was the cocoon.

Oh, Lord.

"I'm sorry," her friend murmured, getting over her shock with some difficulty. "I had no idea—"

"It's not what you think," Branwen whispered back, not wanting to disturb Matthew, if by some miracle he had not yet awoken. He had stopped moving, and his breathing was calm. Maybe he was still asleep.

What could Esyllt see? Heat flooded Branwen and her heart started to beat frantically. The way she was curled up inside his embrace, with her back against his chest, meant that his manhood would be hidden from view. Had her friend realized he was naked by now? The arm resting in the dip of her waist was covered by the blanket, so perhaps it would not immediately be obvious. Dear God, this was mortifying. She closed her eyes, not knowing what to say.

"You need not say anything." She heard something in Esyllt's voice she could not quite place. Was it laughter? Relief? Approval? "Only I see now that you are indeed all right, and have no need of me. Good night."

When the door closed again, Branwen already knew she would not be able to sleep another wink. She also knew she would not wait until Matthew woke up before leaving the bed, and the room. It would be too embarrassing to lie with him while he was naked. And how was she going to face Esyllt tomorrow? Would she tell Connor where his brother had spent the night? No, she decided, her secret, if secret it was, was safe. But her friend would definitely believe they had slept together.

Which they had, of course, only not last night, and not in a bed.

Matthew stirred and mumbled something in her ear, something about a rose and a carpenter she could not make sense of. What was he dreaming about? Unable to help herself, she turned around to bury her nose in the crook of his neck. Mm. So warm, so spicy. His scent was as alluring as he was. If only she could remain in his embrace always.

For a long, luxurious moment, time seemed to suspend its flight and Branwen bathed in masculine perfection.

When a faint glow lit up the horizon, she left the bed.

~

"My lord, the delegation of Welshmen has arrived."

"Thank you, John."

Matthew did his best to hide his irritation. He'd forgotten all about the meeting planned for today, and he could have done without it.

Upon waking up, he'd been disappointed not to find Branwen in the bed next to him, even if it had not surprised him. There had been fresh clothes on the stool, and a tray of food waiting for him on the chest. She had seen to his comfort before leaving the room. But had she left the castle yet? That was what he wanted to know.

Ignoring the food, he'd gotten dressed in the blink of an eye, cursing his exhaustion. After his ordeal of the day before, his body had needed to recuperate. As a consequence, he had slept a lot longer than he usually did, so it was more than possible Branwen would already have gone back home.

But to his relief, he'd found her with Connor and Esyllt in the great hall. She had reddened when she had spotted him, but she had returned his greeting readily enough. He'd been able to breathe then. She was not embarrassed by their night spent together; she would not refuse his company.

Except that now he was told he would be denied the opportunity to spend time with her. Instead of getting to know better a woman who intrigued him more with each passing day, he was going to have to listen to Welshmen blabber on about land borders and finances. He could have screamed in frustration.

"Let the men in," Connor instructed John.

A moment later half a dozen men walked into the hall, none of whom looked familiar. His heart plummeted further. He had made some acquaintances amongst the local lords, even friends of sorts, but none of these men counted amongst the one who'd just entered. Not only that, but they didn't look particularly amenable.

Damnation, he was about to spend the day with a horde of hostile men, when he wanted only one thing, to be with Branwen.

Matthew turned to offer her an apologetic smile—and startled when he saw that she had gone as white as a sheet. Was she about to faint, as she was prone to do? It wouldn't be the first, or even the second time she'd done so in his presence. But there was usually a good reason for it. So what was it? Had the pain in her arm suddenly worsened? She'd said when he'd taken her to bed that it was better, but what if he had inadvertently bumped against her during the night? Guilt sliced through him. He should not have agreed to sleep next to her when she was injured, at the risk of hurting her. Then he frowned, because there was something odd about her reaction.

She was not in pain, he decided, the change in her was too sudden and too extreme. She'd been fine a moment ago, smiling at him sweetly as if remembering lying in his arms. What was happening?

He followed the direction of her gaze. The Welshman facing her seemed the cause of her distress. No, it was more than distress, he amended, it was fear.

She was afraid of the man.

His hand twitched, as if wanting to reach for his sword.

As he was wondering what to do, the man threw her a smile that showed all his teeth. His rotting, crooked teeth. "Hello, Branwen. Long time, no see."

Everything within Matthew tightened. He'd been right, Branwen knew the man. As to why she might fear him, it was not hard to guess. He would be one of the bastards who had once thought to use her for his selfish pleasure, one of the most violent ones, by all accounts. There was intimate knowledge in the way his gaze roved over her, and cruelty in his smile. And if that had not been enough to prove his wicked nature, then there was the terror in Branwen's eyes. She looked about to retch with it.

"How long has it been? Ten years?" he added, when she didn't answer him.

Ten years? Matthew recoiled in shock. How old was Branwen now? Younger than he was, surely. So that meant she couldn't have been much more than seventeen when they had met. Understanding tore through him. The man smiling at her so lewdly was the man who had ruined her as a girl, the one who had started it all.

Blood roared in his veins, making his temples throb. Fate had brought the man to him, thereby ensuring he could avenge her. He would not let the opportunity pass.

"Branwen, would you come with me while the men have

their talk?" Esyllt took her friend by the arm with a smile. "I think Gwenllian will have woken up by now. I know you were anxious to meet her."

Bless the woman. She had seen, as he had, that Branwen was about to retch from fear, and was making it possible for her to escape the man's malevolent presence without incurring offence or creating problems for Connor.

"Yes, wife, go show your friend the babe," his brother agreed. "I fear our discussion will only put you women to sleep anyway."

Ah. So he had noticed Branwen's reaction as well. He would never have been so condescending toward either woman if he had not. He thought his wife a reliable and capable ally and usually kept her involved in discussions regarding the managing of their estate. There was only one reason for him to send her away with such alacrity.

He wanted to give Branwen a chance to recover from her shock away from prying eyes.

Matthew threw him a grateful glance.

As soon as the women left, the men sat down to discuss the matter at hand, but he could not focus. All he could think about was asking Connor who the hell that man was, and dreaming up ways of making him pay for hurting Branwen all those years ago and ruining the rest of her life in the process.

"What's ailing you?" his brother asked, when the men finally departed. Matthew had no idea had long they had stayed. It had felt like forever. "You've been glaring at the Welsh—"

"Who the fuck is that man and where does he live?" he snarled, rounding on his brother.

"Who?"

The question took him aback but then he remembered there had been six men present. "The oldest one, the one with the rotten teeth. As soon as I know who he is, I'm going to hunt him down, and make him eat his cock balls first."

Connor recoiled at the venom in his tone, as well he might. Matthew was not usually a violent man, but in front of the bastard who had raped a young Branwen and ruined her life, he could feel himself becoming a different man.

"Wait. What are you talking about? What did Bryn do to you to get you in such a state?"

"He did nothing to me." He bunched his fists into balls. If only the man preyed on other men, men who could defend themselves. But no, the despicable bastard chose to hurt vulnerable women and children, like the coward he was. No doubt Branwen was not the man's only victim either. He needed to pay—he had gotten away with his crimes for too long. "It's none of your concern. Just tell me where I can find him."

"No. I might not like the man, but I must respect the lord. We need to keep him sweet. He's just granted our tenants access to the sea through his land. This is a significant advantage, an invaluable source of food. Or did you not hear?" No, Matthew hadn't heard a word of the discussion. He hadn't cared. The man could have promised to hand over a chest full of gold carried over by the king himself, he would not have noticed. "So you're not to harm him, not without good—"

"The hell I won't! And if you knew what kind of man your precious neighbor was, you would not want anything to do with him, this much I can guarantee." He slammed his fist on the table, causing the inkpot to spill. Neither man seemed to care. "Damn it, Con, this is not just a whim. I *have* good reasons."

Reasons he could not reveal. Branwen's secret was not his to share, her suffering was not his to use to convince his brother to punish a man who deserved to be punished. He would have to do this on his own.

And do it he would.

Against all odds, he'd been given a chance to make the bastard pay for what he'd done. He would not let it pass. How could he look himself in the face if he did?

He darted to the door. Connor would not reveal the man's whereabouts, but there was no need, for he had given him a vital piece of information. The man was a neighbor with lands bordering the sea. With that and his name, Bryn, it would not take Matthew long to find him. He could have followed him and demanded retribution now, of course, sliced through his gut with his sword, but he knew it was better to resist the urge. Not only was the man surrounded by five burly men at present, but it would be too merciful a revenge.

Much better to let him go while he plotted his next move. Because he didn't want to just kill him.

He wanted to make him suffer and let him know precisely *why* he was suffering.

Chapter Twelve

Branwen would never know what her intentions were with regards to Matthew when she headed toward the east tower, because she was not given the chance to find out. Would she have started another of the whimsical discussions she was so fond of, when he teased her about the meaning of her name or they tried to find out who the skeletons in the ditch belonged to? Would she have revealed more of her painful past to him? Would they have argued, with him calling her a whore? Would she have kissed him and begged him to show her what she had refused to allow herself to feel the time she had taken him in a shocking assault?

She would never know.

All she knew was that she missed him terribly and needed to see him. It had been three days since she'd left Castell Esgyrn as precipitously as if the hounds of hell had been at her heels. She had hated fleeing thus, without even telling him goodbye, but after seeing Bryn, she could not have remained there a moment longer. The man haunting her nightmares had not changed in all these years, only become even more frightening, quite a feat considering how vile he'd been back then.

She had fled, and as a consequence, had not seen nor heard from Matthew in three long days.

If she had been honest with herself—and she would *not* allow herself to be, no matter what—she would admit that she had been hurt by his lack of concern for her. Instead, she'd tried to justify his behavior. No doubt some important business had kept him away from the village, she told herself. Connor would have sent him on some mission or other, and he'd had no time to himself. And, after all, why would he even want to come to her?

She was nothing to him, and he had other things to do than idle his day away talking about white ravens and long-forgotten skeletons.

But still, knowing she might get a glimpse of him, she had not been able to resist the temptation of a visit to her friend and her babe. It was as good an excuse as any to come to Castell Esgyrn. But Esyllt and Connor hadn't been anywhere that she could see when she had arrived, only the two girls. When Jane had told her that her uncle had gone to the east tower, where no one ever went as it was undergoing much-needed repairs, she had allowed curiosity to overwhelm her.

What was he doing there all alone?

She started to ascend the stairs, wondering what she would tell Matthew. He would know she had come to the tower with the intention of seeing him, since no one was supposed to go there. Would he be—

She stopped.

Something like a moan had reached her ears, causing her to trip on the last step. Had she heard right? Perhaps her mind was playing tricks. Why would Matthew be moaning? Then there was a grunt, unequivocally masculine. Her mind was not playing tricks. She froze, her hand on the cold stone. Was he ... was he with a woman? Was that what she was hearing? Was that why he had gone to a disused part of the castle? So as not to be disturbed? Was that why he'd stayed away from the village, because he'd found himself a lover?

Shock sliced through her, then pain and humiliation rushed into the open wound. He'd told her he didn't bed women because he could not take the risk of fathering bastards. Well, evidently, since he'd had her, he'd started to change his mind about that. The virgin had gotten a taste for making love and was now bedding all the women he could find. It would not be difficult, for who would refuse a man like him?

Rooted to the spot, she tried to summon the courage to go down the stairs. The last thing she wanted was to hear Matthew with another woman, hear the pleasure he gave her. But her legs seemed unwilling to move. There was another moan, more sinister than arousing. What was going on in that room? Surely he wasn't taking a woman against her will? Tears swelled in her eyes. Not, not him!

And then she heard it. The sentence that had haunted her nightmares for years.

Gwaranda ar dy cwyno. R'wyt ti'n hoffi be'd 'wi'n wneud, ond wit ty?

Listen to you moaning. You like what I'm doing to you, don't you?

Except ... except that it was pronounced by a voice that did not raise the hairs at the back of her head.

Matthew's.

The ground opened from under her. He was telling his lover the exact same thing Bryn had told her years ago. He was giving another woman what he had not been allowed to give her, and he was praising her response. He was praising her for feeling pleasure, the pleasure Branwen hadn't been willing to feel in his arms. And he was doing it with the same foul words her tormentor had used to make her believe she was enjoying his attentions, to convince himself she had come to him willingly.

It was the ultimate betrayal.

She did turn around then, but then she stilled when she realized he had said it in Welsh. She knew he didn't really speak her language that well—certainly he could never have said such a complex sentence, much less while in the throes of passion. So what was going on?

A muffled cry reached her ears. This time she was certain it was not a moan of pleasure.

"What was that?" Matthew carried on in English, snarling so much she barely recognized his voice. "I can't understand what you're saying. Oh, perhaps you're actually in pain, is that what it is? And you'd like me to stop? You don't *really* like what I'm doing to you, do you? Well, what if I ignored your protests and carried on anyway? What if I carved your heart out of your chest, pretending all the while you're deriving pleasure from it? How would you like that, you sick bastard?"

Another cry, unmistakably one of pain.

Branwen didn't hesitate and rushed into the room. The sight meeting her eyes was not one she would ever have wanted to see. Matthew was bent over Bryn, a dagger pressed against his ribcage. Blood was staining the older man's tunic in various places, bearing testimony to the wounds that had already been inflicted on him. Realization hit. She'd had it all wrong.

This was no tryst between lovers, this was torture.

"No, stop!" she cried out, causing Matthew to freeze. Lost to his rage, he apparently had not heard her come in. His face when he turned to look at her was a mask of fury such as she had never seen before, a fury not directed at her but terrifying nonetheless.

"Why?" he spat. "Why should I stop? Why does this despicable excuse for a man deserve your mercy? Did he show you any when he pinned you under him? When he ignored your protests? When you were little more than a child?"

"No," she said in a whisper. He had not shown her any mercy whatsoever. "But he made a monster out of me, I will not have him make a murderer out of you now as well, do you hear? I won't let him win!"

She fell to the floor and started crying. Instantly Matthew let go of his dagger and knelt next to her, drawing her into his arms. "Sweetheart. I cannot let you say such a thing. Please, you're not the monster here. He is."

The words barely registered, as did the warmth of his body against her flank. She was chilled to the bone, horrified by what she had seen, nauseous at the memory of all that had been done to her. "I ... Please, I just want to go. I cannot bear to see him."

"Yes, of course."

Lifting her in his arms effortlessly, he carried her out of the room, slamming the door behind him with a kick. He brought her down the stairs, and then into another room. All the while, he kept her tight against his chest and whispered soothing words in her ear. She focused on them, using them to anchor her mind in the same way someone who'd stumbled into a crevice would grab at tree roots to avoid plummeting to her death.

After a while she understood that they were still in the east tower. Not wanting her to be seen in such a state or to have to see anyone, Matthew had brought her into another of the disused, empty rooms. There, in the absence of benches or stools, he'd sat unceremoniously on the floor and positioned her in his lap, so he could cradle her against him.

Branwen had never felt so cherished, and finally, the warmth of his body and the comfort of his concern seeped into her.

He'd wanted to avenge her. Not only that, but he'd thought it all out, and gone to the trouble of finding out how to say the exact same words Bryn had told her all this time ago, so that his revenge would be more meaningful, so that the vile man would know how it felt to be ignored when you were in pain, to be told you were enjoying something when you were dying inside.

"Is that what you did these last three days?" she asked at long last. Hunt the man down, learn the complicated Welsh sentence, plan his punishment?

Matthew nodded. "Yes. After I understood who he was the other day, I knew I could not let his crime go unpunished."

Understood. So he had seen her reaction, he'd cared enough to find out the reason, and when he had, he had taken it upon himself to avenge her, all without her having to ask for anything. She was humbled. To think she'd felt ignored …

"I hope you're not angry with me." He sounded unsure.

"No." How could she? No one had ever done anything like this for her. The only people who might have wanted to avenge her, Esyllt and her mother, didn't have Matthew's strength or steely determination. They would never have been able to bring a man like Bryn to heel.

Matthew placed a kiss on her temple.

"Go to him," he breathed into her ear. "Tell him what you need to tell him, that you never wanted him, despite his claims, that he raped you and he knew it. Do to him whatever you think he deserves. Free yourself, Raven, take your revenge. I brought him here for you. This is your battle, not mine."

Branwen felt as if her heart was about to explode. Could it be so simple? Could she free herself, in some small measure at least? "I-I cannot. He will—"

"He's tied to the chair and the chair is nailed to the floor," Matthew growled, sounding as if he regretted putting the nails into the wood rather than into the man's flesh. "He's gagged and blindfolded. He will not look at you, he will not say anything, and he's not going anywhere. He will just have to listen to whatever you need to tell him."

Branwen stayed still for a long moment, considering her

options. How had Matthew guessed that she needed to tell Bryn she had never wanted him, that she had not enjoyed what he had done to her? All these years she'd had to live with the burden of knowing she had been unable to defend herself, and the shame of not having done anything to stop him. He might not care to hear what she had to say or feel any remorse over his actions, but it was not what mattered. She would have said her truth—*the* truth—out loud.

It might help her to heal and give her the strength to refuse the next man who tried to pretend she was willing.

She looked up into Matthew's velvety eyes. His mouth was set in a grim line, and she noticed his jaw was covered with a short beard, as if he'd not even bothered to shave these last few days. He had never looked more magnificent.

"Come with me, please. I cannot bear to go in there alone."

"I will do whatever you want me to do, Raven. Always."

"You swear he won't be able to touch me?"

"He would have to go through me first, and believe me, if he tried, I would—" The rest of the sentence didn't pass his lips but there was murder in his eyes. Branwen nodded. Bryn would not hurt her today.

Slowly she scrambled back to her feet then gestured to Matthew to go first. He led the way, solid and dependable. At the top of the staircase, he opened the door and moved to let her through. She wavered when she saw the hated man crumpled on the chair, suddenly unsure she could do what needed to be done.

Matthew took her by the elbow, providing the support she needed. "It's all right," he whispered in her ear. "I'm here."

Branwen planted herself in front of Bryn. He had tensed, aware despite the blindfold that there were people in the room. He would be thinking Matthew was back and wondering where the next blow would come from.

"It's me, Branwen," she said in Welsh.

Her voice died when Bryn relaxed again, as if thinking he had nothing to fear or even concern himself with if it was only her. Not a promising start. Her eyes flickered to Matthew who nodded his encouragement.

Taking a deep breath, she started talking.

"I never wanted you, not that day in the woods, not ever. You knew it and yet you pretended I enjoyed your caresses. You raped me, and you made it look as if I had agreed to it. You goaded me. You took your pleasure with me and you left me to rot on the forest floor. Now every man I meet thinks I'm a whore he can use for free." Every sentence was said flatly, with barely any emotion, and with each new word she could feel the weight in her chest get a little bit lighter. "I don't hate you, even if you made my life hell, because I don't want to waste any more time on you. I just want to be free of you. You have stolen enough from me already. My innocence, my choice in the men I bed, my ability to feel pleasure, my future with a good man. *You* are the monster, not me. It is enough for me to know that."

The man started to shake. It was such an odd reaction, that it took her a while to understand he was laughing. Laughing! Pure white anger washed through her, making her dizzy. How dare he mock her? He was unable to answer, touch or look at her, but somehow he still managed to make her feel dirty, inadequate.

It was unbearable.

Her hand shot out before she could stop it, before she even understood she wanted to slap him. In the end, her desperation was such that it was more of a punch, one that sent pain shooting all the way up her arm. Because he'd not seen it coming, Bryn did nothing to avoid the blow and received it square in the face.

He stopped laughing.

Branwen turned around and flew down the stairs.

Matthew would have liked nothing more than to kill Bryn for daring to laugh at Branwen when she had been brave enough to confront him, but now was not the time. His death should not be quick, and it was more important he got to her before she could flee like she had the other day. He could not, however, stop himself from kicking the bastard in the groin before rushing after her. The man howled and doubled over.

"Raven, wait!"

He bounded to the door in hot pursuit.

Though he had not understood anything of what Branwen had told Bryn, he had seen her face transform while she'd talked to her abuser, her demeanor become more assured. The confrontation had helped unburden her of some of her helplessness, just as he'd hoped. She might not realize immediately, but being able to voice out loud what had poisoned her all those years, telling him what she had been too terrified to tell him before, expressing what she had truly felt, would, with hope, help her start the healing process. She would now be unable to think of herself as a coward who had not dared contradict the man who'd pretended she was enjoying his touch. Her voice had been heard. Bryn now could not ignore what he had done, even if he'd chosen to laugh it off, bastard that he was.

Matthew bunched his fists. He would pay for that provocation alone later.

"Branwen!" Frantic with the need to see her, he reached the bottom of the stairs. Where was she?

He found her in a corridor to his left. Eyes screwed shut, she was hugging a stone pillar. His heart broke at the sight.

"Here," he said, coming to stand right behind her. "Hug me instead. I'm warm, and I'll hug you back. Please."

She turned and fell into his arms. "Oh, Matthew. That was a disaster."

"No. You were magnificent out there, so brave and strong. I'm so proud of you."

He kept her against him a long time, stroking her hair tenderly, allowing his own heartbeat to return to normal. Eventually she drew back, looking ill at ease.

"I want to go home," she said, staring at the floor. "I don't want anyone to see me like this." He knew what she meant. One look at her and questions would be asked. It was obvious she had cried.

"Does anyone know you came here today?"

She shook her head. "Only the girls. No doubt they will tell their parents I came, but it matters not; you can always say I chose to leave when I could not find them. Please. I just cannot see anyone right now."

"I'll take you back to the cottage on horseback," he decided before she could say she would rather walk. He could not let her go on her own while she was so upset. Fortunately, she seemed to agree she was in no state to be alone and didn't protest. "Where is Silver?" He would not come back to Esgyrn Castle tonight if the dog was not by her side. It was already costing him every ounce of understanding to agree to leave her alone in that moment.

"Still with Mam and Eirwen. He is better, but I didn't think he was ready for the long walk to the castle."

"Then we will get him back before I take you to the cottage," he ruled. "You will want him with you." *He* wanted the beast with her.

There was a pause. When she opened her mouth, he already knew what she would ask him. "What about—"

"Don't worry about him. I'll do what needs to be done."

He would have to talk to Connor at some point, of course, and decide what should be done with the man. He was his neighbor, as he'd said, and they had recently contracted an important agreement. Hundreds of tenants counted on it being honored. He could not go behind his brother's back in such an important matter, and create problems for him, so he would consult with him. In any case, it was better not to rush.

A few nights locked in a cell would give Bryn the chance to mull over what he'd done and Matthew time to come up with a solution to his predicament. If he went to him now, he would only rip his guts out and that would help no one. He needed to come up with a solution to make him pay without anyone else having to suffer from it. What that could be, he wasn't sure at the moment.

Still, that was for him to worry about, not Branwen.

She had suffered enough.

"He's going straight to Esgyrn Castle's dungeon," he concluded. "You won't have to think about him ever again."

Chapter Thirteen

"Someone's waiting for you in the solar."

Matthew stilled. Something about Connor's demeanor made his hackles rise. His first thought was that Bryn's men were here to see him. Somehow, they had found out what had happened to their master, and they had come to demand revenge from their neighbor for what his brother had done. Well, let them try. They would get to hear all about the man's villainy, and if one of them had the gall to defend the bastard, he would find himself having to fight for his life.

He looked at his brother nervously.

Connor had no idea that his supposed ally was this moment imprisoned in the castle, and he would not take it very well to be told. Matthew hated the deception, but he'd had no choice. For Branwen, he would face worse than his brother's wrath. Besides, he was certain Connor would side with him once his neighbor's true nature was revealed. He would want the man punished for what he'd done.

Yes. But how? It had been two days, and Matthew still hadn't decided what the man's punishment should be. All he knew was that he wanted him to suffer.

"Is it someone I actually want to see?" he asked, rubbing a hand over the back of his neck.

The hesitation flickering in Connor's eyes made him rethink his first idea. What if guilt had made him jump to conclusions? What if this was not Bryn's friends but yet another potential bride brought for his consideration? It had been months since his brother had mentioned any noble ladies wanting to ally themselves with the Hunter family, and he had never taken it upon himself to actually bring one for him to meet, but it was all too possible he'd thought it was time Matthew married.

His whole self rebelled at the idea. He could not marry a stranger, a noble woman, someone he felt nothing toward, a Mary or an Elizabeth. He could never be content with such a wife. He wanted a woman he knew, one with origins as modest as his own, someone who made his insides flip in his chest every time he saw her, and with a name as unique as it was poetic.

Of course, he already knew one woman who fitted this description. She also had a smile as bright as a summer's day and eyes the color of the sun illuminating it. Holy hell, since when did he have such fanciful musings? He was truly losing it.

"Well, *is* it someone I would want to see?" he growled, his confusion making him snap.

"Yes. Trust me."

His brother placed a hand on his shoulder. That gesture told Matthew everything he needed to know. The person waiting for him in the solar was not one of Bryn's men, or an elusive bride—but his father. He was suddenly certain of it.

He swallowed. Connor waited, then gave his shoulder a squeeze.

"You need to tell him. He deserves to know."

"I know."

He'd regretted letting the man go without asking where he could find him if the need arose, because even then he'd suspected he wouldn't be able to live with the knowledge that he had willingly denied a man the right to meet his son. And now, against all odds, he was given the opportunity to tell the carpenter what he'd never thought he'd have the opportunity or the courage to tell him.

It was just like it had been for Branwen two days ago. Here was the chance to ease some of the burden he was carrying, to let out the resentment poisoning his life. He would not be less brave than she had been.

"How did you find him?" he asked Connor.

"You have Mortimer, the steward at Sheridan Manor, to thank for this. You know he's an astute man."

Matthew nodded. A very astute man indeed. Growing up, he'd often wished he had a father like James Mortimer. Lord Sheridan had been generous and attentive to his material comfort, but somehow distant, too busy overseeing his vast domains to worry about a little boy he'd taken under his protection. The kindly steward had been more approachable, and taught him most of what he knew. He felt the utmost respect and affection for him.

And now it seemed he would also owe him a reconciliation with his father. But how?

"What did he do?" Mortimer was all the way in England. How could he possibly have arranged a reunion between two people he didn't know were related from so far away?

"He got talking to your father before he left Sheridan Manor, and it didn't take him long to conclude that a man looking for your mother so long after her death might be someone we wanted to be able to trace. He took the liberty of writing to me that very evening to give me all the information he'd extracted from Richard, and in turn I took the liberty of sending Archie to get him in his village."

"Did you?"

The carpenter would have been bewildered by the request, understandably. A mighty lord he'd never met had bade him come all the way to his Welsh castle. It would have made no sense to him. Why had he not ignored the odd request? That was what Matthew would have done in his place.

Unless he'd known why he was being summoned, of course.

He clenched his teeth. Surely his brother had not taken it upon himself to reveal his and his mother's secret without even consulting with him?

"Did you tell him why you'd summoned him all the way to Wales?" he asked less calmly than he would have wished. Nervousness mingling with uncertainty made him look for an easy target, and Connor was here, looking not in the least guilty for what he'd done.

"No. I thought that what we tell him or how was your choice to make. I trust you to make the right one."

With those words and one last encouraging squeeze to the shoulder, Connor left.

Matthew stared at the stone wall for a long time, wondering what to do, or rather, *how* to do it. He already knew he would tell his father the truth, he could not let the man leave a second time without having been told about the son Rose had given him. But what was the best way to do it?

The news he was about to impart would be a shock. There was no knowing how he would receive it. And where would they go from there? Father or not, the man was a stranger to him, they would have to learn everything. Of course they could find out they shared a common passion, had similar views on life, and this this would help make the relationship—

No. He was getting ahead of himself. First, he had to get inside the room and deliver the news. Doubt froze him in place. He was about to tell someone the words he had dreaded to hear all his life.

You have a child you never knew about.

Making sure he would never get to hear those awful words was the reason he had kept his urges in check all these years, the reason behind his iron will, the reason he had never known the pleasure of a woman's embrace before Branwen had forced him to take what his body was craving. How would the man—Richard, Connor had called him—take the news? Would he be horrified? Pleased? There was only one way of knowing.

He pushed the door open.

The carpenter started at his entrance, then gave a nervous bow, as if unsure how to behave in front of a figure of authority. In his velvet tunic, at home in such a grand castle, Matthew would appear like a nobleman to him, as mighty as Lord Sheridan. That gave him the courage he needed. The man didn't deserve to be left in the dark when the person making him ill at ease was none other than his own son.

"Good afternoon," he said, gesturing to the man to straighten back up. "I trust you remember me?"

"Of course, my lord. We met at Sheridan Manor last month."

Matthew raised a hand. "Please. I'm not a lord. I'm ..." He hesitated then said rather bluntly. "I'm Rose's son." Once the admission was out, he found it easy to carry on. The words tumbled out of his mouth. "I know it will be a shock to you, and I have no way of proving I'm telling the truth, save by answering the questions you might have about her. I hope you will believe me."

The man—Richard—his father—blanched. There was a long, excruciating pause. Then he took a tentative step forward.

"Of course I believe you. Your eyes ... the shape of your mouth. They are identical. Dear God. You *are* her son, I was right."

He blinked a few times in rapid succession, as if to make

sure he was not seeing things, or keep tears at bay. Matthew knew he looked like his mother, he'd been told many times. Never had he been more glad of the fact. He now wished someone could tell him what he had in common with the man in front of him, if anything. Did they have the same jaw? Were their smiles identical? Perhaps Connor could tell him. He would have to ask him later. Suddenly he needed to have everyone know the bond linking him to this man, the father he'd never thought to meet.

A good man who had loved his mother.

In front of him, Richard seemed lost in his contemplation.

"I thought you looked familiar when last we met, and I wondered for a moment if you were not her son. But I reasoned you could not be, for not only were you were a grand lord, but you didn't tell me about the connection when I asked about her."

An uncomfortable silence followed.

"I know I should have told you who I was. Forgive me, but your visit took me by surprise, and I didn't find the courage to tell you what I should have." He swallowed. He would not be such a coward again. He thought back to the way Branwen had faced Bryn the other day, saying all that needed to be said and being mocked for it. She'd had to do a much more difficult thing, and he would draw strength from her courage. "I am indeed Rose's son. And ... yours."

Matthew watched as all the blood drained from Richard's face.

"My ... Rose bore my child?" He looked about to collapse from shock. "And I never knew? All this time, I never knew? I wasn't there for her. I wasn't there for you!"

The pain in his voice was too much to hear, the regret in his eyes too much to see. Matthew lowered his gaze to the floor.

"I'm sorry, I don't know what to say."

"Me neither. I'm not sure there is anything *to* say." There was another pause. "Except perhaps ... that I'm glad. I'm grateful for this last, wonderful gift from her. Another son, one I already know I could love, if he weren't so—"

"Please, I'm not," Matthew cut in, already knowing what he was about to say.

But Richard carried on bravely. "If he weren't so much grander than me. I'm only a humble carpenter. How can a man like me ever be a father to you?" He looked around him meaningfully, but Matthew shook his head.

"I'm not grand. My brother Connor is." He would have a lot of explaining to do, Matthew thought when he saw the frown on Richard's face. "He is the nobleman. I am the son of a carpenter and a maid who loved each other, who wanted me, and that means more to me than all the riches in the world. I always thought you had abandoned my mother, and me," he admitted in a low voice, ashamed but wanting to be honest.

"With good reason, because I did." The words seemed wrenched from the carpenter's throat.

"You did not, not in the way I thought at least. That's the important thing."

He could see in this moment that it would be all right. They would get to know and love each other.

"What is your name?" Richard asked tentatively.

It was ridiculous. His own father didn't know his name. "Matthew," he said, his heart in his throat.

"Dear God, that's my second name. I told Rose as much that summer."

Matthew stared at him. That they shared a name meant everything to him. He now had a father and a bond to him, a way of showing their relationship to the world. He remembered Branwen teasing him about his name being uninspiring. Privately, he had agreed, and wished he could have a more poetic name, like hers. Now he knew he had the only name he needed to have. His father's name.

"I think my mother must have loved you," he murmured. Why else would she have called him Matthew?

"And I loved her. She was the most beautiful woman I had ever seen, you know. But that was not even what drew me to her. There was this connection between us, from the start. It is hard to explain if you have never experienced it, but I was convinced from the moment we met that we were meant to be together. I still am." He paused. "Only we were denied the chance to live our destiny."

"That is terrible." Matthew cleared his throat. "I wish ... I wish for both your sakes things had been different."

"Yes. And yours."

"Don't worry about me. Raised at Sheridan Manor, I wanted for nothing." Yes, as the bastard son of a maid, his life could, and should, have been very different.

The two of them looked at each other a long moment.

"I am your father so you will allow me to give you some advice." Richard closed his eyes and gave a rueful smile "If you ever meet someone who makes your heart beat in a different rhythm when you see her, then do not make the same mistake as I did. Do not let anything get in the way of your desire to be with her, even noble reasons. An eternity of regret is too painful. We only have one life. We should be allowed to live it to the full."

"What if I have already met her?" Matthew mused, as an image of Branwen tore through his mind. After he'd taken her home the other day, she'd asked for some time alone, and he'd agreed, reluctantly. It had been two days. In other words, an eternity, during which he'd done little but think about her and waiting for the moment he was finally able to go to her.

Richard seemed to understand all he had not said. He placed a tentative hand on his shoulder.

"If you have already met her, then go get her, son."

In the end, Matthew didn't have to go to Branwen. She came to him. When he exited the solar, intent on going straight to the stables and then on to her cottage, he saw her standing in the bailey, flanked by the faithful Silver. Surely it had to be a sign? He had wanted to see her, and here she was.

"Branwen." He stopped in front of her, feeling more breathless than he should. Admittedly, he'd broken into a run at the sight of her, but he'd done little more than descend a few steps before that. A man in his physical condition should not even have registered the effort.

"Matthew." She blushed slightly, as if she had not expected him to be the first person she would see. "Good afternoon."

Why was she at Esgyrn Castle? Had anything happened, or had she simply come to see Esyllt and Gwenllian? Or ... him, perhaps? Hope swelled in his chest. Had she found the last two days as excruciating as he had? The way she was blushing seemed to indicate her pleasure at being with him, but he could not be sure. She could also be embarrassed by the memory of what had happened the last time she'd been at the castle.

At this moment a groom appeared, leading his white stallion out of the stables.

"Oh, you got Raven back? I'm so relieved." Delight made her eyes sparkle. "I was so worried you would never see your stallion again."

She was so beautiful, her joy on his behalf so honest that his heart skittered—and then started to beat, just as his father had said, in a different rhythm. It was then that he knew.

"Yes. I've finally got my Raven back," he said gruffly, emotion threatening to overwhelm him.

And I'm never going to let her go.

"Was he harmed at all?" She hadn't noticed he'd not been talking about the horse, which was perhaps for the best.

"Not as far as we could tell. Connor's men scoured the country for him, as you can imagine. It wasn't long before they found a destrier hidden in someone's field." Not that it would have been difficult. Even with his telltale color covered with mud in an effort to make him less conspicuous, the powerful animal would have stood out like a sore thumb amongst the nags the farmers kept.

"And the men who attacked you? What happened to them?"

He waved the question away. All that could wait. There was something else he wanted to discuss, something he could not have shared with anyone but Connor and her, who would understand the importance of the news.

He took his hands into hers, and looked straight into her molten gold eyes. Dear Lord, she was so precious to him. He would have to tell her what she'd come to mean to him, one way or another, and soon. But first this.

"You will never guess what happened," he said softly. "I just met my father. He's here at Esgyrn Castle."

Branwen stared at Matthew in wonderment. He'd met his father? What was she supposed to answer to that? After years of doubt and suffering, he'd finally met the man who had sired him. How did he feel? Was he pleased? Angered? Disappointed? Horrified? She knew he'd feared, quite understandably, to learn that his mother had been taken against her will and then forced to give birth to her attacker's child.

Please God, don't let it be the case, she prayed silently. It would kill Matthew to have his worst fears confirmed, and she wasn't sure how she would bear it herself. Her feelings for him were too strong for her to remain unaffected by his pain.

"I'm not sure why I'm telling you," he added, as if he'd read her thoughts. "Only ... I'm so relieved to finally know the truth, and to see that it is nothing like what I had feared all these years. You listened to my story, you know why I dreaded fathering bastards, so it feels right to tell you."

It did. With their fingers entwined, there was this connection between them.

Being with him felt right.

"Do you want to tell me more about it?" she asked hesitantly, hoping she was not taking liberties. To her relief, he smiled.

"Yes, I do. Come over here. Behind that wall, we will not be overheard."

Not letting go of her hand, he led her to a little rose garden just outside the lists. It was a rather sorry sight on this gloomy day, but she enjoyed the shelter it provided from the wind as well as the privacy. Here they would be able to talk without anyone seeing them hold hands. It was a rather intimate gesture, but she would not have let go for all the world.

As they sat down on the bench, a cacophony of barks heralded the arrival of a group of five wolfhounds into the garden. The remainder of Silver's litter, she imagined. The dog, recognizing immediately who they were, bounded in their direction with an explosion of joy.

"Silver seems happy to be reunited with his brothers and sisters," Matthew observed with a smile.

She knew he was stalling, because what he wanted to tell her was hard, so she pretended they were here to talk about the dog.

"Yes, I'm glad to see him so full of life. His injury has finally healed, and after days being cooped indoors, he needed a good run." She watched as her faithful companion bolted toward the forest, followed by his brothers and sisters. How exhilarating it must be to be able to expend out energy thus—not think, and just be!

Soon the barking faded into the distance and silence fell in the garden. Branwen waited, knowing it was not her responsibility to break it. Eventually, his fingers still entwined with hers, Matthew spoke.

"My father is here at Esgyrn Castle. He is called Richard. He's English, as you might have guessed. His second name is Matthew. He's a carpenter. He must be around fifty. He has brown eyes, like me. I first met him when I went to Sheridan Manor, a few weeks ago." Each snippet of information was delivered in a matter-of-fact voice that did not fool her for a moment. He was deeply moved to finally be able to put a name and an identity on the man who had fathered him, as was she. "He had come because he wanted to marry my mother at long last. He had no idea she'd been dead for more than twenty years."

The poor man had wanted to marry Matthew's mother? Shock rooted Branwen to the spot. This was so far removed from what she had expected to hear that she didn't know what to say, or even if she was required to answer. Heart thumping hard in her chest, she waited. Perhaps there would be more information forthcoming.

"This is a lot to take for me, even if it's wonderful. All my life I thought I was ... I feared I'd been the product of a rape, and now, as a grown man, I'm told my parents loved each other and wanted to get married from the moment they met. I thought my father was a bastard who'd abandoned my mother, but it turns out he's an honorable man who wanted to give his son by another woman a decent life."

Branwen wasn't sure she quite followed what Matthew was

saying, who that other woman was, but she didn't interrupt. He needed to talk, confide in someone, and it moved her that he had chosen her of all people.

It would all make sense in time; it was all that mattered.

Slowly, he disentangled his fingers from her, and started to walk back and forth, like a man prey to agitation.

"I don't know how to adjust to the situation. Now I have a family. A father, a half-brother, and even a nephew, would you believe it." He gave a small laugh and she could not help a smile. She knew he often jested about Connor having only ever given him nieces. "Someone who actually wants me."

Those last words were like a punch to the gut.

I want you! she almost screamed, all smiles wiped from her face. *Please don't go back to England now, to be with them. I couldn't bear it. I once had to go weeks without you, and it was awful. I could not do it for a lifetime.*

What had been the best of news for him could well turn out to be a disaster for her. How would she bear him leaving now?

"Lord Sheridan and his wife wanted you, Connor still wants you. You're his only, his beloved brother," she said, instead of voicing out her concern. That was true, at least, and he needed the reassurance. "Esyllt, the girls, they all love you—you must know that."

"Yes, I do. But it's not the same, is it?" His eyes were burning with a new intensity when he finally looked at her. Her heart started to beat a frantic rhythm. What was he about to say? "I want my own family. I'm sure you understand. I need to know I too have someone—"

"My lord?"

A voice cut through his heated declaration. A moment later a man she recognized as one of the guards entered the garden. Matthew turned to face him and snarled. "What is it?"

Branwen started. She had never heard him speak thus to

anyone. Even when he had called her a whore, he had not appeared so menacing.

"Forgive me." The man coughed, understanding he had interrupted a very private and, by the looks of it, important conversation. "But his lordship is asking after you. He says it's urgent. He's in the solar, waiting for you."

There was a pause, during which Matthew seemed to do what he could to regain control over his temper, proving he had been as surprised as she by his outburst.

"Go ahead then," he told the man in a more conciliatory tone. "Tell him I'm coming."

Once the man had left, he faced her again, a dismayed expression on his face, as if he feared she'd been scared by his unwarranted ferocity. The smile she gave him made it clear she had not.

"Will you forgive me? Connor wouldn't have called me if this had not been—"

She placed a hand over his arm. "Of course. I'll wait for you here. Come back once you've seen your brother."

Chapter Fourteen

"You bitch!"

Branwen froze. The venom in the voice, the insult, barely registered. All she could think was that, unlike what she had allowed herself to believe, Bryn was not dead.

And now, here he was, alone in the rose garden with her, where no one could see them and therefore come to her rescue. The timing seemed too perfect to be true. Had he seen her and Matthew come here then waited, biding his time, until Matthew had been called away, to pounce on her? Had Connor even asked after his brother or had it all been a trick destined to draw him away? What was Bryn even doing here? The questions jostled in her mind but she could not make sense of his presence here. How had he even escaped from the dungeon where Matthew had ordered him to be sent?

She had heard footsteps approach earlier, but thinking it was Matthew coming back from seeing Connor, had not thought anything of it. What a mistake! Because now she was trapped.

Slowly, she turned to face her enemy. He looked gaunt, and the beard on his jaw made him appear more menacing than ever. His lips were curled up in a sinister parody of a smile, revealing his rotting teeth. Never had she seen a more terrifying sight. She could have screamed, in fact, she *should* have screamed, but her whole body felt encased in ice. She had thought him dead. Or at least, disposed of, unable to get to her again. She'd been wrong, so terribly wrong. He wasn't dead, he'd come back to her, wanting retribution.

And Silver, the only protection she could have called upon, was nowhere to be seen. She was all alone with a monster, just like that day in the clearing. Her chest felt crushed, as if under a great weight, and there was not enough air in her lungs.

"You've become a fine woman, you know," Bryn rasped, his eyes aglow with ill-contained lust.

Yes. *Become.* Because she had been little more than a child when he had preyed on her all those years ago. Anger flared up inside her, melting some of the ice, allowing her to breathe again. She held on to it with all her might. Being angry was much preferable to being scared. She shot up to her feet.

"What I have become is of no concern to you."

Branwen made to walk past him, aiming toward the only opening in the wall. He blocked her path and she stopped, loath to touch him, even through the barrier of his clothes. She doubted she would have been strong enough to push him out of the way anyway.

She took a step backward.

"So, you now claim you never wanted me." He arched a brow.

"'Tis no claim. I never wanted you and you knew it, but you chose to ignore my protests." Matthew's words came back to her, giving her the strength to speak out. Yes, the ice in her veins was melting fast. Soon she would be herself again, able to think, able to act. "A man knows when the woman in his arms doesn't want to be there."

The laugh that answered her was unlike any she had ever heard, chilling. Far from being chastened, the man seemed amused.

"But of course he does. It is quite obvious. That doesn't mean he should deny himself the pleasure of possessing her, now, does it? It is in the natural order of things. Why do you think God created women weaker than men? It is only so that we can have what we need, whenever we need it, regardless of their ridiculous scruples."

He'd known! All along, he'd known he was raping her, and yet he had chosen to ignore her refusal, derived even more satisfaction from it. All this time, she'd clung to the notion that he had somehow been mistaken, and genuinely thought she was welcoming his touch. How stupid could one get, when they didn't want to accept the truth of something? Well, no more.

Fury broke through the last of her fear.

"You bastard!" Branwen exploded, too incensed to care if he caught her now. What could he do to her that he hadn't already done? "You knew I was just a child! How many more poor girls have you raped?"

"What I do with my life is none of your concern."

"I care not about your miserable life!" In fact, she now wished Matthew had killed him the other day. Why, oh why, had she stopped him? It was not only about her, because as she'd just said, she didn't doubt he was a menace to all the young girls around.

Before she could escape, he seized her by the wrists, bringing her flush against his body. He smelled of sweat and blood and the dungeon where he'd spent the last two days. It took all her inner strength not to be sick.

"But I do care about my life and what is done to me. And I'll make you pay for sending your English pup to me and allowing him to humiliate me the way he did," he growled in her ear, his foul breath hitting her nostrils. She swallowed back bile to answer him with all the malice she was capable of.

"I didn't send him to you. If you got hurt, you've only got yourself to blame. It was only a matter of time before someone stronger made you pay for your vile actions."

"And you think your Englishman did?" Well, by the looks of it, he had. The various cuts and bruises on it made Bryn's face even more frightening than usual. There was no telling what his body looked like underneath his blood-stained clothes. She had seen the knife in Matthew's hand anyway. She knew he had hurt him. "I will repay him a thousandfold for what he did, never fear. I will not let him escape retribution. By the time I'm finished with him, he will wish he had stayed in his country. But first, I'll deal with you."

There was no prize for guessing what he meant. Except this time, he might well kill her after he'd taken his pleasure with her.

No.

The word exploded in her mind. Never again would he touch her. Suddenly she felt strong enough, determined enough, woman enough to refuse a man and send him to hell, if that was what was needed to protect herself and other innocent girls.

Bryn ab Owain had raped his last victim.

Certain of his victory, he didn't seem aware of the change in her. He took a step backward and started fumbling at his braies. "Kneel. I'm going to start by ramming your foul words back in your throat with my—"

Thwack.

Branwen had knelt at his command, but only to seize a piece of rock she had spotted while he was busy unlacing his braies, and she hit him on the side of the head with it, putting all her hatred, all her desperation behind the blow.

"No!" she screamed, while he toppled over with a grunt,

stunned both by the force of the hit and, she imagined, the fact that she had dared stand up to him. "I will never kneel or lie down for you ever again, do you hear? Or anyone else. You cannot make me!"

She struck him again, not aiming anywhere in particular, just knowing she needed to prove to him and to herself that she would not be used again, needed to incapacitate him so he could not hurt her, needed to do whatever it took to stop him. He screamed and tried to get back up, so she hit him again and again and even kicked him straight in the groin, when she felt him crumple at last.

Once he'd stopped moving, she ran toward the opening in the wall—and collided with Matthew, who was coming the opposite way, with Connor fast on his heels.

"Branwen, dear God, what happened?" He steadied her with both hands at her shoulders. "Is it Bryn?"

How had he guessed? She nodded, barely able to push the words out of her trembling lips. "He ... he appeared out of n-nowhere after you'd left. I—"

"*What?*" Matthew roared, as he turned around to look at his brother. This was exactly what they had feared, why he and Connor had been rushing back toward the rose garden in the middle of their discussion. Because they'd feared Bryn's next move.

The reason his brother had called him earlier was to inform him that they had found out the trap door to the dungeon stood open.

"Do you happen to know anything about that?" Connor had asked, suspicion etched all over his face.

Yes, unfortunately, Matthew immediately guessed what had happened. Bryn had escaped, aided by an unknown accomplice. He stared at his brother, knowing the time for the reckoning had finally come. He would have to justify his action, explain why he had taken it upon himself to imprison their neighbor, and he would gladly do it. But now was not the time.

If Bryn was on the loose, he needed to go.

"I will tell you all, I swear, but we have to go to the lists now. Branwen is on her own in the rose garden."

"Branwen? What's that to do with—"

"Now! There's not a moment to lose. I'll tell you everything, but we need to go."

A dreadful premonition had seized him. Bryn would have only one thing on his mind now that he was free. Get his revenge for the humiliation he had endured the other day. And he would deal with Branwen first, the most vulnerable of his two attackers.

He rushed back to the garden where he had left her alone and without protection. Silver was not even around, too busy chasing after his brothers and sisters. Why, oh *why* had he not insisted she wait for him in the great hall, in full view of everyone? The mistake had ended up costing him dearly, because just had he'd feared, Bryn had gone to find Branwen at the first opportunity. What had he done to her? As if he couldn't guess. Didn't he know what the man was capable of?

He yanked at a fistful of hair as despair flooded him. This was all his fault. He should have gone to her sooner, he should not have allowed Bryn to take another breath after he'd mocked her so cruelly, he should not have left her side for a moment, even to go to Connor ... Whichever way you looked at it, it was all his fault.

He tightened his hold around her when she started trembling, then threw a pleading glance at his brother, who instantly stepped forward, one hand on the hilt of his sword.

"I'll go see to Bryn."

Relief spread through Matthew. He'd been hoping to hear

that. The man needed to be disposed of, but he didn't want to let go of Branwen, who was clinging to him desperately.

"He ... I think he might be dead," she said, her voice barely above a whisper. "He was not moving after I hit him, but I did not have the courage to look."

She'd hit him? Brave, brave little raven. He placed a kiss on temple. "You did well. I'm so proud of you."

"Worry not, I'll deal with it, whatever the situation is," Connor soothed. "You stay here with Matthew."

Matthew knew he didn't need to instruct him to make sure the man never rose again. Neighbor or not, there would be no second chances. While they'd rushed to the rose garden, he'd explained briefly why he was so bent on avenging Branwen, and why he had placed the man in the dungeon unbeknownst to everyone. Connor had agreed that the man needed to be punished, so he could rest easy. Before dawn, one way or the other, the vile man would be dead, and Branwen would be safe.

"Sweetheart, talk to me," he urged her once they were alone. Her attitude was worrying him. Was she about to faint? "Did he touch you?" What she'd said seemed to suggest he hadn't, but he needed to be certain.

"No. He said he would make you p-pay for hurting him, and that women were only good for seeing to men's needs, and then he demanded that I—" She stopped abruptly and shivered again. Matthew had no idea how he managed not to howl, because he could guess all too easily what the man had wanted her to do. "So I hit him with a rock. Three, four, five times. I don't remember."

"As long as you did hit him." His next kiss landed on her cheek. "You did what you needed to do, and saved yourself, like you saved me in the forest."

"Yes. I saved myself." That idea seemed to appease her somewhat. She finally stopped trembling.

"Now, let's go to my room."

She nodded in agreement but her legs faltered as soon as she tried to move. Without a word, Matthew swept her into his arms and took her over to the other side of the castle, where his bedchamber was. As he passed the door frame, he thought to how he had dreamed of doing that exact same thing many a night. Only, in his dreams, he brought her here because they were about to make love, not because she had just been attacked by a vile lecher and needed reassurance.

"Stay here, wait for me. Bar the door," he told her quickly. "Open only for me, Connor, or Esyllt, no one else. I'll go and see what's happened with Bryn." The man's name was little more than a snarl.

I hope Connor made him suffer before finishing him off. Better yet, I hope he kept him alive long enough for me to me to cave his skull in and make him eat his entrails.

Branwen nodded, her eyes brimming with tears. She was doing her best not to let fear overwhelm her, and he couldn't resist. He leaned in and kissed her. A tender, reassuring kiss at first, that quickly turned into something passionate, a plea for more, the beginnings of lovemaking. Her hands fastened in his hair, pulling him even closer. His body surged, and he pressed against her, in search of feminine heat, of soothing softness and delicious friction. She moaned her approval, the sound bringing him back to his senses.

What was he doing? Not now, he could not let his urges overtake him now!

Though he would have liked nothing more than to give in to his desire, make her forget anyone else had ever touched her, and tumble her onto the bed beckoning to them, he had to go see to Bryn first, make sure he was well and truly dead this time. He could not allow the threat he represented to Branwen and other women to continue.

Besides, he could not be as boorish as to take her to bed when she'd just suffered a fright. She needed the protector right now, not the lust-filled beast. He had to be strong.

With difficulty, he drew away.

"I'll be back," he said, placing his forehead against hers. "Wait here for me."

"Yes. I too need to know what happened to—"

She stopped before she could utter the hated name. Matthew bared his teeth. He already knew what would happen to the bastard. He would die, like he should have died the other day. This time there would be no hesitation.

"Of course you do. And so do I." He placed his closed fist on his chest, right above the place where his heart was beating as he gave her his solemn oath. "He will never hurt you again, Raven. One way or the other, I will make sure no one ever hurts you again."

~

As soon as he saw the form lying on the floor, hatred overcame Matthew, flooding his veins in one uncontrollable rush. Only one thought remained in his mind. Revenge. All honor forgotten, he rushed out to the Welshman and kicked him in the ribs. The dog deserved no better.

"You piece of shit! How do you like that? Do you want me to make you scream? Is that what you want? Is that what you like to hear?"

"Brother, stop. He's dead," Connor said, placing one hand over his shoulder. The words did not manage to penetrate the haze of fury clouding his mind. He kicked again.

"You are going to pay for what you did to—"

"He's dead," Connor repeated gently. "It's over. He will never harm your woman or anyone else again."

Your woman.

The two words finally got through his rage and he froze, staring at the corpse at his feet. The man was indeed dead. Matthew didn't even ask if Branwen's blows had killed him or if Connor had finished him off. It mattered not. All that mattered was that he could not harm Branwen now.

He fell to his knees, feeling like a failure. "This is all my fault. I should have guarded her better, but I thought—"

Connor shook his head. "It's not your fault. How could you have thought he would escape from the dungeon? It should have been impossible. He obviously had some help from someone at Esgyrn Castle, someone sympathetic enough to the Welsh cause to overrule their loyalty to me. I will need to investigate, for I cannot afford to have such a traitor in our midst."

"No."

His brother had a fair number of Welshmen in his employ, men they had thought trustworthy. A few of them would have come in contact with the prisoner when they'd brought him water and bread over the last few days. Which of them had been swayed by the man's foul ranting, Matthew wondered? He could all too well imagine Bryn spewing his venom through the trap door, telling them they didn't owe anything to the despised invaders. Damn it all, he should have seen to the man himself, or even better, leave him to rot like the rat he was.

They would have to make sure the incident was isolated and they were not harboring a nest of traitors.

"I'll help you," he told Connor.

And throttle the man with my own hands when we find him. Because by freeing him, the traitor had allowed Bryn to find Branwen and almost rape her again. That was an unforgivable offence.

"Yes. Now, go back to Branwen."

"I'm sorry," Matthew said, getting back to his feet. "I know an agreement had been reached between you and—" He glanced toward Bryn, loath to even speak his name.

"I'm not sorry. 'Tis as you said. I don't want to owe people like him anything. I believe his son will honor the agreement, and from what I've seen, he is a far more reasonable man than his father was. Do not give it another thought. I'll deal with the corpse."

Matthew nodded and gave his brother a brief, brotherly hug. "I'll go get Rich—my father to help you. He will keep the secret. It is best if word of what happened here doesn't spread. That way we'll catch the traitor more easily. He won't be on his guard if he thinks Bryn safely out of the way. He might even think his disappearance has yet to be noticed."

"You're right." Connor nodded. "Now go to your woman. She'll need you."

Aye, she would, but not as much as he needed her. He couldn't wait to hold her, and let her know she was safe at last.

He ran back to the bailey in search of the carpenter. Night was falling fast over Esgyrn Castle. Even better. The dark would help with the secrecy. He found his father in the stables, talking to the groom about the best way to skin a rabbit. They both looked sheepish when they saw him, as if caught doing something wrong. For some reason, it amused him. They had hardly been plotting anyone's demise.

"A word with you, if I may."

"Of course." Richard followed him to the gate without question.

"I need you to go to the rose garden just outside the lists and find Connor," Matthew instructed in a low voice. "He needs help. It's a delicate matter, but I told him you could assist him." He didn't want to reveal more, in case they were overheard. Until the traitor had been identified, they could not be too cautious. It could be anyone of the people around them.

"If you think I can be of service to his lordship, then of course I will go."

"I know you can. He will explain everything." He hesitated. "And, father? Thank you."

"You're welcome, son. Thanks for thinking of me."

The two of them stared at each another awkwardly, then slapped one another on the shoulder. Matthew cleared his throat. Dear God, but it felt good to have someone to call father.

And now that he had found himself a second family, one who was related to him by blood, he wanted to claim Branwen as his, make her part of his life as well. Would she agree? There was only one way of knowing.

After one last nod at his father, he ran back to his bedchamber.

"Branwen," he called, knocking softly so as not to frighten her. "'Tis me. You can open the door."

At first he didn't hear anything. Had she fallen asleep? Or was it worse than that? For a dreadful moment he thought she might have left the room in search of comfort, and he would have to go through the whole castle to find her. He wasn't sure his frayed nerves would be able to withstand it. Then at last, he heard the latch being removed. A heartbeat later, he saw her beautiful face beaming at him.

"Oh, Matthew!" She threw herself into his arms. "Are you safe?"

"Me? Yes, sweet, don't worry about me, I'm all right." He tightened his hold over her quivering body. "It's all over. He's dead. You won't have to worry about him ever again."

They remained locked in the embrace a long moment, bathing in each other's warmth and scent. Then he nudged her back inside the room and closed the door behind them.

"'Tis late already, and you'll be tired after your ordeal," he told her, hoping not to let his longing show on his face. "Stay here tonight, in my bed."

This time it was him asking. And to his relief, she didn't hesitate.

"Yes."

Without further ado, she stripped down to her shift before slipping under the covers, as if it were the most natural thing to do, and she trusted he would not get overcome by lust at the sight of her in such a state of disarray. And she was right not to worry.

Though he could not help noticing how beautiful she was, though his body had responded as could be expected at the proximity of a half-naked woman, he knew he would be able to remain in control of his urges. This longing he felt for her was not a carnal impulse.

It was a call of the soul.

Branwen was exhausted, and badly shaken by the events of the day. Right now, she needed security. He could provide that, and he would be honored to. His declarations would have to wait, his lovemaking would have to wait, everything but tenderness and care would have to wait.

With as much ease as she had discarded her gown and shoes, he took off his tunic, braies, and boots and joined her in the bed.

"Come here, Raven, lie in my arms," he said, settling himself next to her. "Where you belong."

Chapter Fifteen

Judging from the darkness wrapping around them, it was still the middle of the night when Branwen awoke. A ray of moonbeam illuminated the bed where Matthew lay next to her, his naked, sculpted, perfect chest on full display. When had he removed his undershirt? Not that she bemoaned the loss of it for a moment, but he'd made a point of leaving it on when he'd joined her in bed earlier, presumably so as not to frighten her. She had thought it odd, considering they had already slept in the same bed twice already, and he'd been bare-chested the first time and fully naked the second.

A smile lit his face when he saw her looking at him. He appeared wide awake. Had he even slept? She wouldn't be surprised if he hadn't. The surprising fact was that after the day's shocking events, she'd managed to fall asleep. But as soon as she had felt Matthew's strong arms close about her, she had fallen into oblivion, comforted in the knowledge that nothing bad would happen to her while this man was holding her.

"No screaming today?" he breathed, his face mere inches away from hers. His now familiar scent, spicy and masculine, as comforting as a hug, wrapped around her.

"No." A smile tugged at her lips when she remembered how she had almost pierced his ear—and hers—the day she had woken up next to him at the cottage.

"Does that mean you're getting used to being with me?"

"It might." So used, she wanted to be with him night after night. "You didn't sleep?"

"No. I could not."

She knew from the strain in his voice that he had spent the night watching her in the moonlight, fighting the urge to touch her, reliving what she had been through in that rose garden. He would be berating himself for allowing Bryn to get to her, but she didn't blame him in any way.

"Why did you remove your undershirt?" she asked, her gaze skimming over the panes of his chest. The man was magnificent. And he didn't seem to be aware of it.

He gave a slanted smile. "Because I was burning hot. I'm used to sleeping naked, if you must know. I made an effort at your cottage and kept my braies on, but today it is spring and unseasonably warm. However, if you prefer, I can—"

"No." This was perfect. Such beauty should never be hidden. Tentatively, she extended her hand—and stopped before she could actually brush her fingers against his skin. It looked warm and inviting, as soft as an animal pelt, with its covering of short golden hairs.

"You can touch me, if you want." When she hesitated, he took her hand and placed it over his pectoral. Holding it just over the place where his heart was beating, he whispered, "Here. Not so scary, is it?"

But it was. Not in the way he meant, but it was. "You know you're the first man I've ever wanted and it ..."

Her voice broke. How could she tell him she was afraid of touching him because then she would want him to touch her? And if he touched her, she might start to feel pleasure in his arms. And *that* definitely frightened her. Would he understand? It seemed such an impossible thing to feel. There was nothing more normal than wanting the person you loved to touch you, to give you pleasure. But because of Bryn and all those men, Branwen had always been afraid of her body's ability to feel. It had seemed wrong, like something she did not deserve.

"I understand. It scares you." He stroked her jaw tenderly. "It doesn't need to. I will never hurt you, never do anything you don't want me to do. You do know that, at least? It would kill me if you doubted it in any way."

"No, I know you would never hurt me." This was never in doubt. The issue was with her, not with him. "I trust you."

There was a long silence during which she focused on the beatings of his heart under her palm, strong and even, soothing.

"Do you think you could allow me to show you pleasure, sweetheart?" Matthew asked, his hand still covering hers. "I know it frightens you, and why. I know you think you do not deserve it but, forgive me, I cannot help myself. I want to make you see that what your body feels can be a beautiful thing, make you understand what it is capable of."

"Will it ..." Her voice trailed, because she wasn't quite sure what she wanted to ask. All she knew was that the offer was tempting.

"I will be with you all the way. It will not hurt, and we will stop whenever you need to. I will not take you, not until you're ready, until you ask me. This is for you, nothing else." He nuzzled at her throat. "Tonight I will only stroke you, if you let me, show you what pleasure is. It doesn't necessarily have to involve a man taking possession of your body. It's something you could do all by yourself."

Yes, she had heard of this, and she had on occasion tried to put her hand between her legs. It had never achieved anything other than make her feel wretched. "I'm not sure that can be achieved."

"It can. I will show you, if you let me."

Perhaps because it was dark, and not daylight; perhaps because the man next to her was talking in English, not in Welsh; perhaps because she was in Castell Esgyrn and not at home, surrounded with the memories of the assaults she had endured; perhaps because she had finally told Bryn she'd never wanted him, for the first time Branwen was able to push her fears to the back of her mind and relax in a man's arms.

Perhaps because that man was Matthew.

Slowly, her eyes hot with unshed tears, she nodded. "Show me."

"If I may, I will touch your hair first."

"My h-hair?" she stammered. This was not what she had expected Matthew to focus on. It was certainly not what she had touched on the rare occasions she had wanted to experiment with her body.

"Yes. Like this."

Strong fingers weaved themselves through her hair and clipped nails started to rake her scalp. He moved his hand slowly, exploring every inch of the sensitive skin covered by her hair. No one, herself included, had ever touched her there. "Ah, yes," she could not help but rasp. This was incredible and, closing her eyes, she allowed the sensations he provoked to bloom inside her.

"What you're feeling is already pleasure, Raven. Don't fear it, you're allowed to experience it."

For a long moment he massaged her in that manner, then he brought his lips to her ear. "Will you allow me to stroke your feet?"

"You want to stroke my feet?" Her words came out slurred.

"Your feet, your arms, your neck, everything. I want to

stroke every inch of you, make you forget anyone ever touched you against your will."

Those men had never brushed her hair or even seen her feet, but he wanted to erase the trace of their touch from her soiled body. It was the most wonderful thing anyone had ever done for her.

"Please," she said, barely able to speak through the lump in her throat.

His fingers, warm and firm, took hold of her left foot. For a long moment, he stroked everywhere, varying the pressure, brushing the instep, circling the bone at the ankle, massaging the sole. A gasp caught in her throat when he took her little toe into his hot mouth and sucked. This was heavenly. He was focusing his attention on parts of her no one had touched, building her trust, behaving as if it pleased him to be touching her thus, and it gave her ...

She started to breathe more rapidly. He'd been right. It gave her pleasure.

Not the kind Bryn had claimed she felt in his arms, not a pleasure sexual in kind, because true to his word, Matthew was not taking her, only making her discover what her body could make her feel. This innocent pleasure she felt she could handle, she could allow herself to enjoy. She felt like a caged animal who'd known only cruelty at the hand of its captor and had finally been freed. Though it was now able to roam free, it was irresistibly drawn to the first kind human it had ever met.

As if he'd guessed the direction of her thoughts, Matthew whispered. "Don't think, just feel. Allow yourself to feel and if you want me to stop at any time, just say so. I will stop."

Stop? No! That was the last the last thing she wanted him to do.

Once again he understood what was going through her

mind. "If you want more, I will give it to you. If you want me to touch you somewhere else, I will."

"What about you?" she managed to croak.

"Me?" There was a growl. "Oh, I'm having such pleasure right now. You smell so good, you're so soft, so beautiful, you feel so good in my hands."

While he lavished compliments on her, he carried on massaging her feet. And it was not long before Branwen wanted …

"More," she said in a rasp. "Please, more."

"Your leg?"

"Yes."

"Can I lift your shift?"

"Yes." She didn't even hesitate. "Stop asking, I trust you. Do what you wish."

"Very well, but remember, I will not do anything you don't want me to do. I will stop whenever you need. You won't even have to ask me … I will feel it if you tense up."

"Matthew, please. Don't make me beg. I could not do it. But I promise you I want this."

"Sweetheart, so do I." His hand traveled up her leg, leaving a trail of fire in its wake.

"Oh," she said when he reached the sensitive skin at the back of her knee. "Oh," she said again, when his fingers skimmed the inside of her thigh with infinite delicacy.

Everywhere he touched felt reborn, cleansed. When his palm covered her most secret place, she said the word she had never said when a man had put his fingers there.

"Yes."

Go slowly, Matthew kept repeating to himself. *You don't want to scare her, not now, when she has gifted you with her trust.*

Never had he felt his responsibility more keenly. The last thing he wanted to do was to frighten Branwen or cause her to recoil in shame when he showed her how much he appreciated her reaction to his caresses. He knew why she would be wary of feeling, or worse, expressing her pleasure. That bastard, Bryn, had used her moans of protests and sobs of pain as proof that she enjoyed his assault.

He knew different, of course, but he understood why she would feel unable to let herself go.

A more unlikely couple he could not imagine. The virgin whom everyone assumed was an indefatigable seducer of women and the victim of abuse whom people mistook for a seasoned harlot.

His finger glided through wet silk. Ah, so her body was responding to his ministrations. And his ... his was about to burst.

"I thank you for the gift you're giving me, sweetheart, the most precious I've ever been given." He lay next to her, so he could speak in her ear while he stroked her intimately. "I hope to repay your trust with the pleasure you deserve. I wish you knew how good it feels to have you in my arms, so warm and willing. You're the first woman I have ever lain with, and I want you to be the last."

He was not sure what he was saying, all he could do was keep talking and focus on making his caresses as delicate as he could. This, at least, he was not new to. By necessity, he had only ever touched the women he desired in that way, and he had learned what gave them the most pleasure. He was confident in his ability to coax a response from Branwen with his hand, even if he would have preferred to do it with his mouth. That would have to wait, however. For now, he could not risk shocking her. They would have to take this step by step.

Under his skilled fingers he could feel her melt and quiver. She was close, even if she didn't know it, even if she thought she could not access the pleasure her body was capable of.

And then he heard it. The most beautiful sound in the word. Branwen moaning for him, allowing him to hear her pleasure, allowing herself to feel—and express it.

He almost stopped, not knowing what to say or do. This was a turning point in her life and he didn't want to ruin it. Should he acknowledge what was happening, and risk making her self-conscious or ignore her moans and make her believe he had not understood the significance of the moment?

In the end he decided to join her. He let out a series of low grunts and whispered endearing terms in her ear, licking the lobe, tasting her, kissing her. To his delight she responded immediately, moaning even louder, pressing herself against his hand.

"Yes, just like this, sweetheart. Let it come. You're beautiful. So beautiful." And then he knew exactly what he could say to show her how much he appreciated her trust. She had bared her soul, conquered her fears for him—the least he could do was reciprocate, bare himself to her. "I love you."

The three little words hurtled her headlong into what he knew was her first orgasm. It was fierce, and almost triggered his own. To feel her spasming around his finger was the single most rewarding thing he'd ever felt.

Then she stilled, while her body recovered from its long-overdue release.

"You love me?" There were tears in her beautiful eyes, tears he wiped away tenderly.

"I do. And I love that you let me know how much you love what we're doing."

"You are going to make me cry," she complained, hiding her face in the crook of his neck. "But I don't want to cry, not now."

"You do what you need to do."

He felt her nod slowly against his neck. "I ... I want you to take me."

Everything within him surged. His heart leapt. His nostrils flared. His cock, already hard, jerked. Nevertheless, he had to be certain they were not rushing things. He had not meant for this to happen tonight, but when she was ready.

"We don't have to do this. I can pleasure you all night if you prefer." His hand landed on her hip. He would not even feel he was missing out.

"No. There is a heat inside me telling me I do want more, I want ... *you*. Please, Matthew, make me come with you inside."

It was his turn to still. How on earth was he going to make her come before he erupted? As soon as he slid inside her wonderful heat, he would come. It was inevitable. Her words had sent him perilously close to explosion, and now he was asked to do something he wasn't sure he was capable of at the best of times. Matthew had never used his cock to pleasure a woman before, and he had no idea how to do it. It was not as if being a skilled lover was an innate skill. It had taken him time to understand how to move his fingers, where to touch or how fast to swipe his tongue, and he had become quite proficient at it. But he'd had no practice whatsoever at taking a woman. How could he ensure he pleased Branwen on his first try?

Never had he felt his inexperience more keenly.

"Love, I would like nothing more than to make you come around me, but I'm not sure I will be able to. You know ..." He might as well be honest with her, as he knew she would not mock him. He placed his forehead against hers. "You know I've never made love to a woman. Last time, you were the one who took me. To my shame, I didn't do anything."

No, nothing, except almost pass out in the most explosive

release of his life. He didn't want that. Tonight he wanted to make sure she was satisfied.

"I've never made love to a man either," Branwen answered, looking at him straight in the eye. "This is new to me too, and I'm not sure how I will handle it. Nothing that happened to me with the other men bore any resemblance to it. But I want to try, with you."

With those words she sat up and removed her shift in one bold gesture.

How could he refuse her now?

"Then we will learn together."

Kissing her as if his life depended on it, he settled himself between her spread thighs, and placed the tip of this throbbing shaft at her entrance. Though strictly speaking it wasn't the first time he'd felt her heat around him, it was the first time he was in charge. It made a world of difference.

He pushed in, inhaling as a sensation, almost too acute to be called pleasure, pierced the small of his back. With some effort, he bit back the series of curses wanting to spill from his lips. He could not let it out, fearing it would cause him to spill his seed at the same time. He had to control himself. This could not be over before it had even started.

He withdrew slowly, feeling resistance all the way, as if Branwen's body wanted to suck his right back in, and never let him go. He plunged back again, and again, faster each time, deeper each time.

"Yes!" she mewled.

And all at once it was too much. The heat was too much, the tightness was too much, the joy of hearing her moan was too much. He came, pouring all that was good inside her.

Then he collapsed.

After such a powerful release, Branwen thought she would not have the energy to move, but when Matthew gave her a luxurious, lingering kiss that made her tingle all the way down to her toes, her sensitized body responded immediately. She blinked. How had she turned into such an insatiable woman?

"I'm sorry, love," he mumbled, "but you felt too good."

"How is me feeling good a problem?" she managed to say through the haze of satisfaction.

"Because this possession was too quick to satisfy you." He kissed the side of her neck. "I told you, I'm too new at this. I wish I were a more accomplished lover, the skilled lover you deserve." Another light kiss landed on her collarbone. "I wanted to make it last, to make it good for you."

What was he talking about? Did he really think it hadn't been good? Although, now that she thought of it, he was right. It had not been good, it had been so much more than that.

It had been a rebirth.

Taking advantage of her stillness, Matthew slowly licked one nipple, then the other, before drawing it into his mouth, and sucking on it languorously. Branwen lay there, unable to move, only able to enjoy the attention he was lavishing on her. How could he think she would want him any different? He was perfect the way he was.

"Just like last time, it was too quick, and I didn't see to your pleasure." His lips followed a path to her stomach, leaving a trail of fire in their wake. Incredibly, desire bloomed anew in her body. Oh, she *had* become insatiable! How was that possible? Surely she'd had enough by now? "But unlike last time, you haven't fled, you're still here in my arms, all soft and warm." He tongued her navel in such a provocative manner that she felt herself go red to the roots of her hair. What was this man doing to her? His every action was provocative. "And I'm not going to let you go until you've reached your release."

Her release? She inhaled. "But I already—"

The rest of the sentence was lost in a croak because his

mouth, which had been hovering above her hipbone, covered her intimate folds. They were still throbbing from his possession and slick with their combined releases.

Never had she imagined anyone doing anything so scandalous.

"Matthew?"

"Branwen?"

"Are you ...?"

"Am I ...?"

She almost laughed at his whimsical answers, but she could not laugh with a man lying between her spread legs and his mouth so close to her core.

"Matthew!" she repeated, in shock this time, when his hot tongue licked a path along her seam. What was he doing? He'd kissed her there, and that had been wicked enough, but now he was *licking* her!

"Do you mind if we carry on this riveting conversation later? Right now, I want to feast," he said, his voice hoarse with desire. That sound caused her insides to spasm, as if to appeal to him. "Ah, you taste divine, my love. Of you, and me. Of my woman. No one but me is going to touch you ever again, no one but me is going to hear, taste, or see your pleasure."

Nothing he could have said could have moved her more. Nothing he could have done could have aroused her more. Her body, which had been sated a moment ago, started to feel empty. As if he'd known, he slipped a finger inside her, and then covered her quivering flesh with his lips. Heat seared her.

"Matthew!"

"Yes, that's me. Let me make you come, in my mouth this time. Let me have your pleasure again. I had my turn, now it's yours."

After that he stopped talking and used his mouth to bring her to the pinnacle of ecstasy. It happened with dizzying speed.

Everything spiraled out of control and burst in an array of light. Or was it heat? Or was it joy? Branwen couldn't tell. All she knew was that her life would never be the same again.

"Matthew." A sigh.

"Is my name all I'll ever hear coming from your mouth from now on?" he drawled, laughter and love dancing in his voice. "I don't mind."

She didn't even have the strength to smile back.

∼

It was obvious from the way Branwen blinked at him when she woke up that she hadn't realized she had fallen asleep after their lovemaking. Matthew's heart melted.

"How long have I been asleep?" She sounded so aghast at the idea of having overslept that he couldn't help a smile.

"Long enough to let dawn pass," he said, nuzzling at her neck. "I was still lying down on my stomach with my mouth between your legs when you dropped dead."

Her face went crimson at his vivid description. "Why did you do that? I had no idea such a thing was possible."

That did not surprise him in the least. None of the bastards who'd taken her to bed would have bothered offering her this gift. They had been guided only by selfishness and lust. Had he been too bold? Should he have waited until she was more familiar with what her body could do to pleasure her in that way? It had been a very intimate, wicked thing to do to a woman who was not aware it could be done, especially considering he'd only just fucked her. But he had been wild with the need to make her come.

"Would you rather I hadn't?" he asked, lifting himself up onto one elbow. "If you prefer, I won't—"

"No!" She sounded horrified, as if the idea of him never

using his mouth on her again was too dire to contemplate. No wonder. He'd yet to meet a woman who didn't like being licked thus. "I loved it. All the same, I cannot help but wonder why you did it."

"I told you. I didn't want to be the only one to reach my pleasure, like the last time."

Damn it all, he would have to learn some control. He was a man of thirty summers, not a lad of thirteen! He could not get carried away thus, he owed the woman he loved satisfaction in his arms.

"But you weren't the only one reaching your pleasure." Branwen flushed, and he loved her for an admission he knew would not be easy for her to make. Up until last night, she had been afraid of feeling pleasure.

"Yes, I know, I saw to it that you climaxed beforehand, but I—"

"Not only beforehand. It also happened when you ... didn't you feel it when you were inside me?"

Matthew was stunned, because no, he hadn't. All he'd known was that he'd suddenly been seized by the need to empty his seed inside her welcoming body. He groaned, flopping onto his back, as he understood that the spasms of her climax were what had triggered his own. And he'd missed it, thereby showing his inexperience and lack of knowledge as a lover.

Bloody bleeding hell. Could this get more humiliating?

"Please, Matthew, look at me." Branwen came to drape herself over him, her slight weight barely registering.

"I feel so wretched ... I wish I were the lover you deserve."

She placed herself so close to his face that he had no choice but to look her in the eye. "Listen to me, English. You *are* the lover I deserve, the only one I've ever wanted. You are perfect the way you are, generous, patient, understanding, and passionate."

Oh, he was that. But he was also untried in many ways. "I mean, I wish I had more experience so I could—"

A light finger landed on his lips, silencing him. Branwen looked uneasy but determined to get her point across.

"Forgive me if you don't like what I'm about to say, but I don't regret you being inexperienced. I like the idea that you were a virgin before me, I like that we are learning this together, I like that I'm the only woman you ever possessed. It makes me feel unique." She blushed an adorable shade of pink, and suddenly he felt like the manliest man in the world. "I was never anything but a receptacle for men's lust, men who might well have been more experienced than you, who had bedded scores of conquests and yet didn't have the skill to please a woman or the inclination to do it. You made me come three times, when it had never happened to me before, once with your fingers, once with your mouth, once with your—"

The part she hadn't dared name reared its head, as if to indicate it was ready to service her again.

"Aye," he growled, drawing her to him possessively. "I did that." It had been beautiful.

She smiled when she felt how hard he was under her, then bravely carried on. "So I fail to see what more you could have done."

Is that a challenge, Raven mine?" With a jerk of his hips, he quickly reversed their positions so he was the one trapping her under his throbbing body. "Then you should know that Connor always told me my left arm was just as strong as my right, and I believe I have teeth that could be put to good use as well."

"Ah, I see." Her eyes twinkled. "Do you mean to spar with me, or eat food in bed, perchance?"

"There will definitely be some rolling around and nibbling involved," he warned, nipping at her earlobe, the action mirroring what he would do to her core the next time he got his mouth on her. "Because you're all mine now, to have, to hold, and to devour."

He started to do just that. Dear God, he could have nibbled at her for hours. She was soft all over and she tasted so good ... His mouth trailed along her neck, in search of her breast.

"Matthew?"

"Mm?" He knew that when she started to call his name thus, it was a good sign. It meant that she was losing her mind. But this time she sounded ... somewhat diffident. He drew back to look at her, ever conscious of not frightening her. "What is it?"

She hesitated. "Where can this go?"

"I can think of only one place."

Marriage, of course. How had she not guessed it?

A shadow passed over her eyes, dimming the gold. "But you know I've been with all these men, what I did to them, what they did to me. You cannot possibly want to—"

Matthew silenced her with a kiss as fierce as he could make it. He could not afford to let any doubt linger in her mind. He wanted her, regardless of what had happened. Her past was her past, unfortunately he could not change it. But her future would be his.

"I can and I *will* do what I want. What I need. I know you didn't go to these men of your own volition and in any case, I care not. Even if you had gone to them willingly, it would not make me want you less. I told you, I love you. Nothing can change that, least of all a past that we cannot change, no matter how much we would like to." He closed a hand over her perfect breast, the gesture possessive. "You are mine, Raven, and you had better start accepting it because I will never stop trying to make you see it."

This was the most moving declaration Branwen had ever heard. Her heart melted, her body heated. How was it possible that this man wanted her after all he'd heard about her, after all he'd seen?

"Oh, Matthew, I love you too, I want to be with you too. But there are so many obstacles in our way."

"Name them and I will shatter them one by one." He threw her a warning glance. "And the first one had better not be the number of men who abused you. You already know how I feel about that."

Though it was a concern in her mind, she saw she would only pain him by mentioning it. "Eirwen ... I cannot just disappear out of her life. She needs—"

"Eirwen will come live with us, of course."

Live with them? Was he serious? "Why would you burden yourself with a—"

This time he stopped her with a finger on her cheek. "Hush. I am doing no such thing. It is no burden to have your sister with us. She is not a simpleton who would bring shame upon me, in the same way that you are not a whore ready to cuckhold me at every turn, but a wronged woman." The crude words were meant to shock her into acceptance, she knew, and she loved him for it, for fighting for them, for not letting her doubts or what people might say get in the way of their happiness. "You are the woman I love, and she is my sister-in-law. Or, at least, she will be when you become my wife."

"Your wife?"

"Well, would you like to be?"

"I would like nothing more but—"

"No but. That's settled. You've allowed me to love you, you've allowed me to show you pleasure last night. Now, will you please make my life complete and marry me?" He paused, his face deep in concentration. "*Wnei di fy mhriodi?*"

"You ..." She laughed through her tears. Who would have thought Matthew Hunter would ever ask her to marry her, in

Welsh no less? She still remembered their first encounter, when he had mocked her and Esyllt for speaking a barbaric language. "So you really are learning Welsh?"

"I am, for my sins. It is a fiendishly difficult language." He pursed his lips. "Only for you would I attempt something like that. I hope to be well compensated for my trouble when we are married. Because, in case you didn't know, the proper response to the question I asked you is 'yes', not 'so you really are learning Welsh?'."

"But ..." How could she agree, even if she wanted to? It was not all about her. He'd asked her to name the obstacles to a union between them, and she would. "You know what people will think when you marry me," she said under her breath. "You will be mocked at best, goaded at—"

"Let them think what they want, I care not. But if anyone ever dared open their foul mouth in front of me, they had better be prepared to hear exactly what happened to you while I rip their bollocks off their bodies."

"I ... They might not all be men," she said weakly. Some of the most violent comments she'd heard had been uttered by women. It seemed that there was no compassion to be had, only ill-placed jealousy.

He cradled her face in his hands, a smile flowing on his lips. Her heart flipped over in her chest when she saw how utterly untroubled he was by the prospect of marrying her. He was not lying to reassure her. Her past really did not matter to him, the jibes he would face really did not worry him, and he really was prepared to offer her sister a comfortable life, and her the family she had always wanted.

It was too good to be true.

"Branwen, look at me. I love you, remember? I told you as much when I was stroking you last night. Poor love, you might not have heard me, what with what was going on between your legs." How could he tease her so? Of course, she'd heard him, that was what had pushed her over the edge. It had given her the reassurance she needed to let go of her fears and allow pleasure to flood her body.

"I did hear. I do remember."

"Then you must understand that I won't have anyone making you turn away from what we both want and deserve. A chance at happiness and a loving family."

"I won't." Her voice wobbled dangerously. "But I don't know how I could bear it if our children ever got to hear about me and what I did to—"

"Not what you did, what was done to you. It is not the same at all. *You* have nothing to be ashamed of," Matthew cut in, as fierce in his defense of her as ever. She melted. With this man on her side, she could face anything.

Perhaps ... perhaps he could offer her what no other man she knew could. A life away from pain and humiliation and the people who would always think her no better than a whore. Here was the opportunity to start anew.

"If we married, would you take me away so we can live in a place where no one knows me? Where I could meet people without fearing them recognizing me? Where I was in no danger of meeting men who had abused me?" She bit her bottom lip, realizing the enormity of what she was doing. It wasn't fair to ask him such a thing. "Forgive me, of course, you might prefer to stay here with your brother. I understand."

He nuzzled at her neck. "Connor has his own family now. He doesn't need me. But you do, and you are my priority now. I will do whatever makes you comfortable. We'll go back to England, to Sheridan's Manor, if it pleases you. I can look after my brother's affairs there, which I'm sure he'll appreciate, because I don't see him spending much time there, now that he has a home in Wales."

"You would do that, after having already saved me?"

"I didn't save you, sweet. You saved yourself, by being brave."

"I love you."

"So say you will marry me. I'm afraid I won't be able to breathe until you have."

"I will. You're my life now."

The kiss she gave him would leave him in no doubt about it. And if the fierceness with which he returned it was any indication, he shared her feelings a thousandfold.

In that moment, everything was perfect.

"I've changed my mind, you know," Matthew told her when they finally drew away. "'White raven' is the perfect name for you. Not only are white ravens as striking and as unique as you are but you have the white here." With those words he kissed her stomach, where the skin was the color of cream. "And the raven there." He ruffled her intimate black curls and smiled. "But you never told me Branwen could also mean 'beautiful raven'."

"No." She blushed. "It sounded presumptuous, I suppose."

"Not presumptuous at all, only very apt. When we have children, I'd like them to have poetic, beautiful Welsh names."

When.

That one word caused her heart to beat faster. Could she one day, with this man she loved more than anything in the world and who, by some miracle, loved her back, get what she had always thought would be denied to her? If only.

"If you gave me what I have never dared hope to have," she whispered. "I'll leave you to decide their names."

"No." He kissed her stomach again, swirling his tongue in her navel. "We'll decide together. Always. But right now, I feel the need to nibble at something delicious."

She stretched and allowed a wicked smile to touch her lips. "Shall we ask for some sugared almonds to be brought up then?"

He let out a growl. "Oh no, I want something much softer than that. Something delicate, and fragrant, and all mine."

Branwen's scandalized laughter was soon transformed into screams of rapture.

Epilogue

Matthew stared at the ceiling above, feeling blessed above all men. In just a few days, he'd gained a father, a brother, a nephew, a sister-in-law, a mother-in-law, and a wife. In other words, a complete family. It was a bewildering development and he had never felt happier.

He looked at Branwen, lying on her stomach by his side, her glorious hair fanned over his pillow. His heart constricted in joy at the notion that this woman was now his to comfort, pleasure, and protect. His to love and be loved by. They had been married for three days and had barely left his room or gotten dressed in that time. The only exception had been when Connor had informed him that he had finally unearthed the traitor who had freed Bryn from his cell. Matthew had been only too glad to punish him, as it was none other than Eric, the guard who had used Branwen so selfishly at the back of the stables.

She was right, it was better if they went away from all the men who would remind her—and him—of all she'd been through.

He'd promised her he would take her to England and Sheridan Manor, and he would honor his promise, but he'd been unable to find the time or energy to organize anything. He'd been too busy making up for lost time, discovering all the treasures his wife had to offer in bed and showing her what her body could feel. At this rate, he didn't doubt they would welcome their first child before the end of the year.

He smiled to himself. All the better if they did. He could not wait to give her what she had never thought to have.

"Matthew?" Branwen stirred.

"*Cariad?*" Since he'd started learning Welsh in earnest, he always made a point of using the endearment in that language, especially when they were in bed.

"Is it morning already?"

"It is." He chuckled when she groaned. She sounded exhausted, and no wonder. Last night's lovemaking had been particularly vigorous. It had not taken him long to learn some mastery over his body and ensure he rode her until she couldn't utter a sound.

"Do I have to get up?"

He placed a kiss on her naked shoulder. "No. You stay here, have something to eat, and I will go see about the arrangement for our ride back home." She made a face he could not quite decipher. "You still want to go?"

"Yes, but …"

"Tell me." Had she changed her mind? He nuzzled the crook of her neck, inhaling her skin where both their scents lingered. "Please, do not hesitate to tell me what's on your mind. Ever."

"I would like to ask Mam to come with us as well," she said in a rush. "You know she's not my real mother but she's looked after Eirwen and me since we were young. She might say no and prefer to stay in Wales, but I'd rather ask her in case she could not bear the idea of us both—"

"I will come with you to the village to ask her," Matthew

said, cutting her fumbled explanations short. He should have thought she would want her mother with her. "I will not deprive the woman of her two daughters and not even ask for her permission beforehand. You know my father will be coming to live with us as well. We cannot have me reunited with the family I always wanted and have you be without the only mother you've ever known."

"Matthew." She sighed as she nestled herself closer to him. "Why are you being so good to me?"

"Because I love you. Because you are being good to me too. Because I only ever want to see you happy." He could have given a thousand reasons, none of which could have explained the fact. "And who knows? Maybe our two parents will find an accord. They are of an age."

"It would be difficult. Mam doesn't speak a word of English." Branwen giggled. "And I assume your father can't speak Welsh?"

"No. But people can learn, you know," he answered in his new language.

"They can. I love you, husband, you know that?"

"Fortunately for my sanity, I do. Now kiss me, wife."

When he came to lie on top of her, she took in a sharp inhale of breath. "I thought you wanted to go and see about our departure?"

"I do and I will." He gave her nipple a long, luxurious lick until it was as hard as the shaft between his thighs. He would go and get everything ready in good time. For now, though, he had other plans, plans that involved making his wife swoon with pleasure. "Later."

A Second Chance for Carys
Read about Carys and James

About the Author

As far back as I remember, I have been attracted to the Middle Ages, to knights in shining armour and their ladies in spectacular dresses. Now I get to write about them, I feel like the luckiest woman in the world. Being French and married to a Brit makes each book I write extra special, as our countries share a long and sometimes painful past. But in the end, in life as well as in fiction, love conquers all!

I have published several medieval romances under my own name, including series, and also have a pen name, Judith Falcon, for spicier projects, still in historical romance.

Join my newsletter and check out my other books on virginiemarconato.com.

Also by Virginie Marconato

The Welsh Rebels
A Husband for Esyllt

A Savior for Branwen

The Noble Norsemen
Taming the Wolf

Soothing the Beast

Wooing the Devil

Baiting the Bear

Tempting the Saxon

Seducing the Warrior

Loving the Blacksmith

www.ingramcontent.com/pod-product-compliance
Ingram Content Group UK Ltd.
Pitfield, Milton Keynes, MK11 3LW, UK
UKHW040254200225
455254UK00004B/166